SistaGirl

by

Anondra "Kat" Williams

ISBN-13: 978-0615853611
ISBN-10: 0615853617

DEDICATION

To all who said I could...
To her for being her, while loving me...
nothing more, nothing less

CONTENTS

CONTENTS

CONTENTS

Anondra Williams

I'm a southern girl with southern sensibilities…

The following words are a homage to the southern women and Mississippi heat that shaped me into the woman I am today…

"Mississippi thick girl"

SistaGirl

No one really gets our friendship. Not that I'm asking them to but you know humans always wanting to understand something that doesn't require understanding. It just is. She's my friend. Not one of those since-diaper friendships, one of those grown-woman we-chose-each other friendships.

I can't even say we met at a club, job or school. Nope we met at a local sandwich shop. She was ahead of me in line and taking way too long to decide on some damn meat bread and vegetables. So I ordered for her, even paid for it. She ate it and we've been friends ever since.

I can't even say we were good friends or great friends from jump, 'cause we weren't. We just strung each other along being casual friends, till one day I looked up and realized she was the person I called when times were good and bad. When I wanted to giggle and cry, she was it. She was also the person I called when that asshole dumped me for that skank from his job. I was the person she called when that skank left Her for that tramp. I'm still pissed about that, her leaving Her.

Yes, she left Her. And that's where the confusion comes in. Most folks think we have to be fucking, sucking or licking instead of well…just being friends. All because I'm straight as straight can be and she's as gay or lesbian as she can be. Whichever term you prefer. Don't make me no never mind 'cause I call her sistagirl and she, she answers.

It doesn't help that she is one of them obviously gay women. Please don't send me no hate mail, email or texts asking me what gay looks like. It looks like her. Now what?

She's attractive ain't gonna lie but then again so are a lot of my friends, hell I'm pretty damn fly myself. And that's where her girlfriends, partners, significant others, whatever you want to call them, had a problem. Hell society had a problem, so I can't really blame them...too much. Every time we hung out alone, her past girlfriends had a problem and thought we were doing something they would do with her besides eat..out. Don't let me happen to call or text my sistagirl late at night, it was World War 3 up in there!

Don't think it was just her girlfriends, the men in my life felt the exact same way. Something to be said for folks so caught up in they own bullshit of what they would or wouldn't do that they can't recognize that everyone ain't them. I told my men friend, I'm grown and I'm gonna do what a grown woman does. Me being alone with her don't indicate nothing more than that. Anyone who protested too much I eventually left alone, they either can't control themselves which means they think I can't either or they been run through the mud so much by other women that the baggage they carrying is too much for me to help with. I give'em two options: take them bags to the nearest dumpster or take them on home with ya, either way don't bring them up in here no more. In the end they were scared she was going to give me something they couldn't. Turns out they were right. She gave me love and friendship. They couldn't.

Lucky her, my sistagirl finally got a woman that understands and accepts our friendship. Loves it actually, loves me. I like her. I'm slow on that love stuff. You know, lesbians so damn clingy, all that hugging and kissing every time you see each other. I told her I don't need no hug every time I see her. Her and sistagirl ignore me.

So yea, she's my sistagirl and we are friends to the end, not that diaper friendship, that grown woman, I chose her and she chose me friendship. I think I'ma go call my sistagirl, I need a few laughs right about now, maybe even shed a few tears as I tell her about my search to find what she's found. She's my sistagirl and I, I love her.

Sometimes…

Sometimes it's the oddest of things that make you stop in the day to day of living. I had been doing things on rote for so long that when I paused it took me a second or two to recognize it. It, I think, was the scent of it or maybe just the change in the air flow as it passed. Either way I raised my head, seeking what wasn't there before, before today or yesterday or last year.

She was beautiful. Surprised, I wasn't expecting a she. But beautiful she was, not in the Hollywood style of beauty, more a southern girl that you take home to mama type of beauty. Started thinking of the Goldilocks and three bears, height just right, shape just right…now if the voice matches the rest then I might have to start believing in fairy tales again.

Wasn't sure how I was going to hear the voice but it appears my good luck or fairy godmother was working overtime today. She spoke as she was passing, a polite stranger eyes meet type of hi. I responded with "Hello beautiful." That made her pause, stop as a real smile appeared on her face as she responded around a grin "Well, I wasn't expecting that, thank you."

"You're more than welcome, but it's true. You're beautiful. I'm sure you've heard that more than once today, yesterday…every day."

"No, I actually haven't."

"You should hear it. You might need to change those around you, so that you hear it daily."

"Really? Hmmm, you might be right."

"I was right about you being beautiful" I said laughing out loud.

Big grins exchanged as words petered out and life moved around us. Finally she says "Well, again thanks. Have a good day."

"I will and you do the same" I said around a slowly fading smile and the realization that beauty was walking out of my life. Then again, what was I to do to her, for her if she were to stay? I'm straight, hell she probably is to. Maybe we were meant to be good friends. Though my reaction to her wasn't girlfriend friendly by any stretch of the imagination. I wasn't one of those women who complimented her friends, told them they were beautiful. I barely a managed a "you look alright, now let's go" to most. Thinking on it, I didn't have many close girlfriends.

All these thoughts flitted through my mind as "Beautiful" walked away…slowly. I didn't stop her and she didn't stop to look back, smile again. She didn't look back and give us both a reason to smile again, speak again, pause again. So we didn't.

Months passed, and I saw her in my dreams, heard her voice when others spoke, felt her smile, even smelled her when others passed. I was finally awake, thanks to beautiful, life was living me or rather I was living it. Finally, awake to other possibilities, chances and I embraced them all. I had been in denial for months, years, a lifetime about who I was, what I wanted.

I had spent the last 30 odd years pretending that the reason I wasn't happy was because of my momma and her issues. Everyone shouldn't have kids. Then it was school and its issues. It's hard to work, get good grades and be better than the rest. After that was the job, have to do more as a black woman than anyone else. In between all this were the black men and all their issues, neck roll, sucked teeth and all. I wasn't putting up with their foolishness. At least that's what I told folks who asked why I was single or couldn't seem to keep a man.

Finally I was honest. I didn't want one, a man that is. I wanted a woman.

Momma didn't act surprised when I told her. I told everyone who would stand still long enough to listen. It was like I had to sing it, shout it "Hey world I'm a LESBIAN! Did a lil jig an all. Called it my "I'm a lesbian cheer and shit."

Being honest no one acted surprised when I told them, though they did keep asking me to do that cheer. I think they laughing at me but that's another story. I'm still not sure why they weren't surprised, it wasn't like I was dating women on the side or in the dark. I was only dating men. Few and far between but I was dating them. I even had a boyfriend through most of high school. Boys in college only wanted you if you were giving up the goodies. I wasn't. I wanted to but the few experiences I had with the high school boyfriend convinced me that sex was overrated.

Soon as I came out as they call it, everyone and their momma had a cousin, a sister or friend to hook me up with. I accepted them all. I was open, wide. Who knew there were so many lesbians out there? Like right there, around the corner, sitting on the block, even at my job. Apparently they were just waiting on me to figure it out, figure out I was one of them welcome me to the "family."

I dated one fine business woman type, had her stuff together on paper. Over dinner she says "I prefer to sleep with women I'm interested in rather quickly. You know, to get the preliminaries out of the way." She also told me in that same conversation that women can't pass anything to each other, that there were no STD's in the lesbian community. I believed her till I started itching and burning, down there. Thankfully it was curable. She didn't care for me telling her she needed to get tested. I didn't care for her giving me gonorrhea, so I guess we were even. We stopped dating while I was undergoing treatment. I told her cousin. Figured she might want to know that before she "hooked" up the next woman.

I learned slowly while exploring. Dating a woman wasn't all that complicated once you accepted two truths. Everyone who is saying they are looking for love, ain't and those looking for love, probably don't love themselves enough to recognize love when its pimp slapping them in the face.

I don't know what I was looking for, I was still figuring out self. I think a part of me was looking for "beautiful" in every woman I saw and dated. It took a year or two for me to realize she wasn't going to reappear, that no one had her smile. Some came close, others didn't appear to even try.

Then I met her. Her was Michelle. Michelle of the bubbly laugh and breath taking smile that lit up a room when she entered. Everyone knew Michelle. She was the poster child for being a black out and proud lesbian. She taught me, what that meant.

Our love started slow. One quiet morning after, I realized I didn't want to leave. It was a Saturday or a Sunday. I was rolling over to disentangle myself before departing, she was sleeping soundly on me. I thought that was odd. I can't stand for anyone to be up under me when I sleep. Feel like they are stealing my air, the good air. Turns out we had been snuggling the entire night. That made me pause. Pause long enough for her to wake up.

"You leaving?" she asked with a sleepy voice, eyes half open, breath barely stirring the good air around me.

I opened my mouth to respond with a yes but instead said "No, not yet. Do you want to grab breakfast somewhere?" My question shocked her. I could see it in the eyes that were now wide open, sleep fading. I had spent the last few weeks jumping up and out as soon as the sun appeared in the sky. Limits in place to keep everything "right".

"Uhmmmm sure, let me jump in the shower first. I know this great spot off Tucker that you would like."

Slow love. It grew.

She got sick and I took care of her. Made soup and purchased boxes and boxes of Kleenex, the kind that didn't smell. Took her temperature every three hours just to make sure it wasn't increasing while pouring Tussin and Nyquil down her throat. She got better.

I think I moved in around that time. It was easier to care for her if I stayed there, at least that's what I told her and others who asked. I had been lucky so far and hadn't experienced the "Lesbian Uhaul" experience. I didn't think it really applied after six months.

Slow love. It grew.

We decided that having kids after being together two years was logical and that we were meant to be together. Forever. She also told me she was going to love me better than I loved myself. I believed her. I believed in beautiful.

I believed till I smelled her again. Another random day, not quite on routine but enough that she made made me pause, breathing in and out slowly. Enjoying and debating, debating on speaking again. It's been five years and I had hoped I had moved past that particular scent. Guess not.

"Hello beautiful".

she left

she left
and
she didn't come back

i wasn't surprised
not much
expected
her desertion
from the first whispered
in the dark

i
love
you
between legs
silent tongue
lips parted

i knew she would leave
and never come back
i didn't stop her
didn't detain her
with promises of change
of hope
of we can do betters..

of love
because
i
knew
she

would leave

i knew because i wasn't there
from the first whispered
in the dark
i love you
between legs
silent tongue
lips parted
i was gone

bidding time physically
while mentally
emotionally
i was down the street
midnight train to georgia
never been before
not that ride
not that train
but this one
this one whispered
in the dark
i love you
between legs
silent tongue
lips parted
i'd been here before
done that
back scratched
heart weary
soul blackened
love had been

i knew she would leave
and i help prepare
her journey
while packing my own bags
i left her
leaving me
i knew she would leave
she left me
but not before
I left me
part of me
behind

Freedom

She asked for it and I gave it. Not easily and not without tears shed on my part. I still wonder on hers, tears that is. The rest was no wondering at all, she was pretty straight forward when she came home that Friday night in late May.

"Hey, can we talk?"

"Sure, you want chicken or fish tonight?"

"I'm not hungry and I don't want to do this anymore."

"Hold up, you not hungry?! Let me write this down." I joked, mainly because the last part hadn't clicked yet. Then it did. "You don't want to do what anymore?" I asked with dread filling me from the inside out, heart racing, mind trying to catch up.

"This, this relationship and it's not you, being brutally honest I've fallen in love with someone else and I want to be with her."

I stared at her for what felt like hours, days even but in reality wasn't more than a minute or two. Stared and processed my life ending. Stared at the woman who just yesterday, this morning said she loved me and this afternoon is saying she loves another. I kept staring almost in a dream, really a nightmare, as she balanced from one foot to foot, body wary as if expecting a strike. I wouldn't hurt her, would never hurt her or any woman. That's finally what made it all sink in. She had never feared me before and now, here she stood fearful of me, the woman who loved only her.

I said "Okay". Really what else do you say to someone who just said they don't want you, don't love you and in fact just told you they love another? You say nothing, as you walk out the door, remembering to breathe with each step as the pain lashes you like a hot whip dipped in hot fish grease from the inside out.

I eventually returned after driving around for hours, realizing I had nowhere to go. Home had been with her for the last three years. I had friends but I wasn't ready to hear or see their shock nor field their questions. So I went back home to the woman who no longer loved me, the woman who loved another.

We didn't speak over the next few weeks, not verbally. Texts and emails escorted me into the land of the newly single. She told me via text that I should leave, move out, sooner rather than later. She told me via email, the name of new love. I told her when I was leaving, moving sooner than later. Luck or fate smiled on me in the form of an offer from my employer to move to a different office, an office overseas in Germany. I jumped at the chance to no longer breath the air she inhaled or the opportunity to see her and new love together.

So I left, packed up and got the hell out of there. It hurt still. I didn't see her the last week I was in the house. Assumed she was hanging with new love. I didn't tell her I was leaving the country. Why? She didn't love me. Why tell her about the realization of our plan, our dream really to live in Europe. Exploring castles, sipping wine in a Parisian café while pretending we were above it all. Guess I would be doing it solo. And I did. I fell in love with Germany and France and Italy, even Poland. I visited them all over the next year, solo.

I heard from her via email a few times after I left. Simple stuff regarding items left behind. You know the typical do you want this type of stuff, then it turned into if you don't pick this up by XYZ date it was going in the trash. I never responded. I didn't delete them, didn't delete any of her emails. Instead I moved them to a folder titled "Freedom". I figured one day when I was ready I would hit the big delete button and symbolically flush her out of my heart…my soul.

Not my life, nor my memories. I was a better person with her. I grew with her, learned about loving with her and yes, learned about heartbreak with her. Still I wouldn't trade one day of it. Life is full of yes's and no's and maybe so's. She was a yes in my eyes...at that time in my life.

Today after a year of learning to breathe again, to smile and mean it, to laugh and enjoy it I get another email from her, the first one in six months. I hadn't read the last one sent to me, just moved it to the folder titled "freedom". This one I read. Curiosity killed the cat and all that. It didn't kill me but it hurt, old scab pulled off still bleeding underneath wound, new blood flowing to the surface.

She wrote to tell me, she still loved me. That her and new love only lasted a few months. She told me she didn't know why she did what she did, cheated, fell in like not love. Bored possibly. Scared maybe. Stupid, definitely. She said she was sorry. And...she repeated that she loved me and only me.

That last line keeps playing in my mind like a black and white movie. For the last hour as I stood on my balcony staring out at the traffic and people as they passed. Moving on with their lives, like I finally thought I was doing with mine. What I thought she was doing with new love.

For over an hour I had been asking myself

why. Why did I open that email. Even more importantly why did I care anymore? Why a part of me, not sure how big, was happy that she realized the mistake she made in letting me go.

I finally stopped starring, went back to the computer, moved the email to the "freedom" folder and then I did what I should have done months ago, I deleted that folder. Time to move forward, I thought as I got up and walked out to the front door, keys in hand. Freedom, I finally have it.

Hit Harder

I hit her
a few times
she wasn't the
first

I hit her
because it's
what
she
deserved

sit, jump, rollover

She didn't
do it
quick enuff

Training her
to do
better
hit her
harder

She will learn

Like I did
at the hand
fist
of my first girlfriend
who taught me
well

And I promised
that I would
love her

The way I was
taught
adding my layers

So yea I hit her
she deserved it

can't cook,clean
right

Watched my daddy
teach my momma
who taught me
when he wasn't around
who taught me
when he was around

Do wrong
hit harder

And I aint
worried
cause she know
I only do this
cause
I love her

Only hit her

to
help her
do better
hit harder

To help her
do better
hit harder

Roses

Roses are red
Violence is too…

This is what I think every time I see the flowers that line our living room table. Roses purchased as an expression of her asking for forgiveness. They were once one of my favorite flowers. No more. She gave me one on our first date. I still have it, pressed and dry between the pages of a book. Symbolic.

The number of roses has increased over the years. Two roses on our first six month anniversary, three on our first year. Half a dozen after we moved in together a month later. Six months after we moved in together, I received my first dozen roses.

The occasion was her first apology for hitting me. A slap and a shove really after I got in her face, at least that's what she stated in her apology as she handed over the flowers.

I accepted.

Three months later I received another dozen. This time there was a slap, punch and a shove. I was told I have a smart mouth.

I agreed.

The flowers appeared quite regularly after that. She started to have them delivered, with a simple note attached. I'm sorry. My co-workers thought it was great, but they didn't see the carefully hidden bruises. Didn't understand why I didn't smile when they arrived or why I started giving them away.

Something I never expected or had ever experienced before her. Two thumbs up for women loving women, women beating on women, each other. She stopped verbally apologizing. I stopped verbally accepting. I did start hitting back. Surprised her and me. Simply got tired of the beatings. The licks, occasional slaps and shoves quickly escalated to full on beat downs from both sides. Don't get me wrong before I hit back, plenty of time passed. Plenty of me begging her to stop, plenty of me pleading with her over vases full of flowered apologies. I begged her around bruised and swollen lips.

She promised of course. Don't they all, till the next time. After a while she stopped promising or even justifying. Really though is there ever a good reason to hit the person you love? When I hit back the first time, it was more of a shove back, get off me type of move. Still it was my first. Symbolic. It didn't stop her, in fact it made the licks that followed more brutal as she cursed at me for "hitting" her.

I took it. That time and even the next time and each time after till it was harder and harder to take…till I didn't. In the middle of her punching me, I punched back, hard. Just as hard as her, just as hard as she punched me. That made her angrier, that I "hit" her again. She started hitting me more, I returned every blow.

This, I considered our first fight. The others were, simply put, beatings. This was the first fight of many. We almost developed a routine. Every other weekend, something I said, didn't say. Something I did, didn't do would set her off. I could see the buildup occurring, first she would start verbally attacking, then items in our home would start flying. Eventually fists would start flying.

At first we fought til she got tired. She started to get tired quicker and quicker and I hit back more and more, harder and harder. Then we fought til I got tired. Finally we fought when I wanted to fight. When she did something I didn't like, said something I didn't like, fists would fly. I got a perverse satisfaction from hurting her, from seeing the tears fall down her face as she begged me to stop. Pleaded with even and I continued till I get tired, til I felt like we were even. Though I know we will never be. There is no even in abuse. There is no even in this house anymore. That chance went away with the first push, shove…bruise. Continued to fade with the first apology given and accepted, followed by the second one, third one.

So here we sit, battered and bruised staring at each other over roses surrounded by tulips, my apology to her. Symbolic.

joker, joker, deuce, deuce

Kat is my name
and
women are my game

hold up that's not what I meant

Kat is my name
and
living life is my game

yea that's more like it

though the game is
playing me right now

hopscotch all over my ass
with big rocks
and the girls
the girls
they wearing heels
and landing hard
as they try
to reach
the number
ten
spread legs

I tried to play jacks
but couldn't
pick up enough jacks
no matter how hard

or how high
I bounced that ball
balls

played hide and go seek
which at times turned
into hide and go get

either way
I wasn't found
not by the one
I wanted
and what I found
I didn't want
I did get it though

It being tired
So I figured I would try
double dutch
hopping and skipping
with two vs one
was…stupid

on my part

jumped in smiling,
thrown out crying
as I learned that
two isn't better
than one
at least not for me

so here I sit

playing
I
declare
war
with myself

after a harrowing
game
of solitaire
no jack, no queen

wishing
I was playing
spades
with a partner
who understands
what

joker, joker, deuce, deuce means

Middle

She sleeps in the middle of our bed. She sleeps in the middle or our bed when she's happy with me, content with us. She sleeps with her face resting below my right breast, inhaling me and us. She says it's the perfect place to sleep. Who am I to correct her as I lean in and align her to me, thigh to thigh, right foot, laying on top of left. Slightly awkward but it's how we fall asleep. Touching, rubbing as she warms me and I cool her.

She sleeps in the middle of the bed because she says it's the only way she can sleep now. Now that we are together, every night in reality of, not limited to dreams. She sleeps in the middle of our bed connecting us and growing us in our sleep like plants, we sprout.

Til we don't.

She sleeps on the edge of our bed. Her side, closed in by pillows and extra sheets that have multiplied in thickness from three nights before in a bed that has grown from king to supersized king, extra width and shorter. My feet trailed the edge as my body searched for comfort and warmth that wasn't there or rather wasn't near.

Arms hanging off the sides not sure what to do with themselves as they are usually busy now, attached to hands that rub absently along curved back, occasional breasts and soft afros. The last two nights, she has crowded the edge of the super-sized king, on her side fighting a silent battle with an unworthy opponent, me.

I conceded the second night, though she didn't acknowledge the white flag of me asking was she hot or cold, did she want hot tea or cold water. Monosyllabic "no's" thrown over turned shoulders as she grips the edge of the bed and pulls her anger around her, mixed in with the chocolate of our sheets, melting.

Tonight I waved the white flag again. She accepted the hot tea over shoulder still turned slightly. Lights out brought silence, spoken thick with promises and apologies coming from both sides of the great divide. As the darkness quiets and settles in I moved slowly to the middle of the bed, fitting myself to her curves. My left arm sliding casually around rounded belly, fingers spreading as they encircle the core of her, tips reaching. Warmth reaching out to encircle my coolness, thighs touching, as I bow down to lay my head in the curve of her neck and shoulders.

I sleep in the middle so that she understands, I'm sorry and that my love for her is deeper than this anger, misthoughts and misdirection. Holding tight as she allows me to inhale her, us.

friday kind of love...

I want a
friday
kind of love
hot
sticky
wet
room filled
with the musk
of her
fingers
reaching
lips
searching
for openings
not yet invented
teeth meeting
bites of flesh
licks of
skin taste testing
lighter here
sugar there
salty on the back
of knees
in folds and creases
of woman
breasts hanging
swaying as nipples
more erect than before
scream
for attention
legs spread

and we
dive
in
seeking
friday
kind of
love
sex
fucking
calling
it all names
as long
as it's understood
we both seeking
a friday only
kind of love

How You Get'em

church

My grandmother always said, "How you get'em is how you lose'em". I took that to be some ol black folk stuff brought over from slavery that didn't hold rightly true. Well at least not til I lived it.

I met her on a Sunday, after church. Not my church, hers. That makes a difference. My church was one of those everyone who wants to worship can come, dressed in however and as whatever. Again makes a difference. Hers was one of those black folk's only churches and by that I mean "straight" black folks only. Single sista's searching for the man God done promised them and single brotha's liking being pursued by the sista's. Mixed in there of course are the couples with kids and the occasional in the closet choir/music director.

I was visiting because a co-worker swore I would feel happy there, get some blessings. I think she thought her church could turn me from my evil ways. My evil ways being me loving women. I went because outside of that I honestly liked her and figured what's one Sunday out of my life. I should have respected myself more and her less. Life lesson learned.

So anyway after the customary welcoming, singing and begging of funds. On a side note why is it all black churches constantly have a building fund offering? I digress but I really want my five dollars back since I'm never planning on coming back again. Anyway after all that, I'm hanging around the front entrance trying to sneak out and avoid the sideway glances of interest that are shown to every new face and figure. My co-worker magically pops up with her in tow. I hadn't noticed her before, too much going on to notice but I was definitely seeing her now. Beautiful dark African goddess, those were my first thoughts. Something about a beautiful dark skinned black woman that makes my heart stop beating and my mind get to wondering. What does that skin taste like, bittersweet possibly...

I stopped thinking on tasting long enough to be introduced to what turns out was my co-workers best friend. She had mentioned her many times when sharing details of her weekends and now I had a visual to match the name. Michelle, Chelle for short.

"Toni this is Michelle, my bestie!" my co-worker sang out loud adding with a laugh "And I saw you trying to escape, but I wanted ya'll to meet before I let you get out that door."

Michelle moved forward while extending a

hand and sharing what I would later term "that smile."

"The famous Toni, nice to meet you finally. She said she was going to get you here one day, come heck or high water."

I shook her hand, while making eye contact and squeezing slightly. I'm nothing if not confident. Her eyes widened slightly as I gave more than the usual weak grip that women usually share. "Nice to meet you as well Michelle, also known as Chelle."

"Ah.. she's told you all my secrets huh?"

"Well not all but quite a few."

"That's good to know, a lady has to have a few secrets. Makes life interesting don't you think?"

"I certainly do…I certainly do."

By then my coworker was standing there with a slight puzzled half smile on her face and a what is going on look in her eyes. "Well now that that's out of the way, Toni how about you join us for a late lunch? I've been wanting my two favorite folks in the whole world to meet and all of us to hang together."

I hadn't planned on doing anything but attending church and heading back home but after meeting Michelle also known as Chelle I was down for anything. "Sure, I don't have anything planned."

Michelle hesitated slightly before saying "Let me check on Mike and the kids first, if they are good then sure why not."

Damn talk about cold water thrown smack dab in your face. I forgot that in all the stories told about the weekend there was the occasional mention of a husband and kids. Oh well lunch still shouldn't be bad, I'll have some nice wet dream stuff for later.

How You Get'em

lunch

Lunch was fun, I guess. I was sitting with two black women who wanted nothing more than friendship from yours truly. Yay me. It passed leisurely as they discussed things and people I didn't know. I spent most of it texting this chick I had met at the club last night. I was planning on stopping by after leaving this lunch, also planning on eating something besides fried chicken. The mention of my favorite artist finally caught my attention. Chelle was mentioning the gallery that would be displaying her work next week and how she wanted to attend. Hmmm, so not only is she beautiful, she has good taste as well. Great. Yay me.

I interrupted their discussion with a "She's my favorite, I've got tickets, you should come with me to the opening next Wednesday." I surprised everyone at the table with the invite, including me.

The co-worker quickly tried to kill whatever the invite implied. "Well I'm not a fan, so I'm going to pass plus next Wednesday is our monthly after work drink and dine with the ladies so neither one of us can go."

"Well I wasn't asking you, I was asking Chelle, matter of fact I still am since she hasn't said no yet."

Chelle took her time answering as co-worker stared daggers at me and sent questioning stares at her. "Sure, I'll go. Missing one drink and dine in three years for some art isn't a bad trade off, matter of fact, I know it's not."

"Great, meet me at the door at 7:30, the gallery opens at 6:00 but I want to go home and change clothes before attending. Unless you want to do dinner beforehand? If so there's a nice little Italian place up the block from the gallery." I jumped in quickly before the co-worker could shit on my date with Chelle the goddess.

"Dinner sounds nice as well, let's do that."

"Cool, sounds like a date then, let's do dinner at 6:30 at Antoine's, and I'll just bring something I can change into at work."

Lunch ended rather quickly after that with the co-worker looking highly pissed. I was content. I had an after-church date with chick from the club and a date of sorts with Chelle on Wednesday night. Life was looking good.

Yeah I know she's married. I haven't forgotten "Mike and the kids" but hey we both grown, what happens, happens.

How You Get'em

date

The week passed rather quickly with the co-worker giving me the cold shoulder til Wednesday where she tried to intrude on my date with her friend Chelle. Can you believe she said she was thinking on going and maybe that would change her mind about the artist? Yeah right. I killed that shit quickly.

"I only have two tickets, I think they have tickets available for Friday or Saturday night, try Ticketmaster." I really can be an ass sometime.

The image of her sourpuss as she walked away made me laugh for the rest of the day. Really what did she think I was going to do? Convert her bestie to a carpet muncher on one date? I'm good but not that good. It doesn't hurt that I'm not bad looking, hell some would consider me good looking. As you can tell I'm easily distracted.

I changed into something slightly more comfortable at 5ish and left work for my sorta date with Chelle. Anticipation in my step, possibilities in my brain. A brain that was quickly overloaded as I laid eyes on Chelle once again. She was beautiful in a beautiful way. Yeah I know that sounds sappy but that's exactly what I thought. Just downright beautiful. I was captivated as I greeted her at the opening of the restaurant. Even more so as we learned each other over pasta and red sauce. She was a reader, a writer and an all around lover of words. Married, of course, with kids. Happy with her life but looking to stretch her boundaries. We clicked. Simple as that, I felt like I had known her forever and wanted to know her forever. Looking back, that was the moment I fell in love.

We talked for what seemed like days but was in reality mere hours as we ate and then viewed the art which though amazing, didn't hold a candle to her. Finally the evening was over but our affair was just starting.

How You Get'em

affair

It started out simply enough after that first date, that wasn't a date. Texts and emails, sharing stories of life and love. Meeting up again for brunch on a Saturday when the husband and kids were otherwise occupied. Dinner on a night when she told him she need some air. I was that air and she inhaled every chance she got. Sucked me in and I fell, head over heels in love with a married woman. She didn't make me, didn't beg me or even coerce me. I willingly jumped up and down in the air for this.

This turned into three years of me accepting bits and pieces of her. A weekend here, a day there. I accepted it all while begging for more of what I knew she wouldn't give. She loved him, her kids and her life. I was her "beautiful surprise" or so she told me. She told me so many things over the years, even told me she loved me. That's what kept me going, whenever I said I was done, whenever I was alone on a holiday and swearing this would be the last one she reminded me of the love she had for me and I for her.

And I loved her, had to. I had to love someone that I gave up living for, waiting on her, waiting on moments with her. Once, maybe twice a week, an hour or two, I gobbled them up and built a relationship around them. Sex we had it, I craved her and she me, we had it a lot. She would walk in taking off her clothes or telling me to take mine off. Soon after she would leave, leave me naked, wet and with the scent of her covering my skin and sheets.

Her husband wasn't a bad guy. We became friends. Shitty of me, but what she wanted. A reason for me to be around at times when I shouldn't be. Family celebrations. I was there. Birthday parties for the kids. I was there. I was the new best friend of wife, aunty of kids who weren't kin. I played my role well. I played and played til one day the tears wouldn't stop coming after one of her walk-in, walk-out visits. I had noticed the last few times we had sex, I cried. I assumed at first it was just my love for her deepening. This time I acknowledged the truth, I acknowledged that I was crying because I was hurt, being hurt, hurting in a half ass piece of nothing, with a woman who I knew would never leave her husband for me. Who would never let me be more than a friend of the family. A friend of the family she occasionally fucked. I still didn't leave.

I cried for the next year as I begged her to leave him for me, told her I could supply all that he did and more. She said no. She said yes. She said a lot of things, anything to get me to stay in her life till she was ready to leave him because in the end she said she would. I believed her. I believed her even when I started seeing her less, believed her when she said work was kicking her ass, the kids were requiring more as they moved into being teenagers and he, he just wanted his wife around. It all made sense. Till I saw her and her together, doing Saturday brunch on a day when he and the kids were otherwise occupied. A day she had told me she couldn't come over, wouldn't come over but maybe another time. Same thing she said last weekend and the weekend prior.

I stood and stared and thought, granny was right, how you get'em is how you lose'em. I confronted her. She said I was too much, wanted too much, that I didn't really understand her and the commitment she made to her husband and kids. She told me I didn't understand my role in her life, so she found someone who did...again. Turns out I wasn't the first and most certainly won't be the last. All the while I thought her best friend, my co-worker, was trying to keep me from her she was trying to keep her from me. I lasted longer than most. Me the player, who thought the love was real. The only real things were the wet stains after a night of her fucking me and possibly fucking him.

That was two years ago, I see her in the streets every now and then. She's got another friend now, friend of the family.

kids

she got kids
and they bad
and good

bad or good
she got'em
and they
were here
before me
after me
if i'm believing
what she saying

no threats
or promises
reality
they hers
and his
he's present
black man

and i get
that she
found herself
afterbirth
secondbirth

and i get
that he's cool
and still has
feelings

but not in
that way
for her
mother of
his seed

and i get that
the kids
the kids
are adjusting
to me
learning me
trying

and me
i'm recognizing
what i've known
from the beginning

i don't want kids

Saturday Mornings

I miss my momma, well not really my momma, though I do miss her. I miss the women she had around her, the friendships she developed over the years of my childhood. The women who came over on Saturday mornings to sit a spell over a cup of coffee, they would arrive early at 7am, ready. The women, who while sipping coffee, had Saturday morning conversations revolving around men, children, work of course other women, always other women. How these other women were messing with their man, how these other women were fucking with them at their jobs, all these other women.

I would sit and listen as insults and slights, real or imagined, were discussed over cooling cups of coffee and rising inner temps of misplaced anger, depression and tiredness. These women, my momma's friends, were always tired. They were tired of struggling, tired of working for nothing, tired of no good men and bad ass kids, just tired. I was one, sometimes, but never on Saturday's. I was the fetcher, the bringer, the turner, the good kid. The one my momma told me I better be on Saturday mornings or come Saturday afternoon there would be hell to pay.

These women who I fetched for sipped on

hot coffee and told tales of being super women, though in their eyes it was just being. Stories of how they got their rent money together at the last minute without selling their souls or bodies. Tales of how this kid or that kids life was spared by the grace of God or because the belt slipped out of her hand at the right moment. I was in a few of those stories. These women told stories of the light bill been past due, but the lights still on. Miracle. Stories of how two or three pieces of chicken feed five. Second coming.

And always a man, whether he done good or bad. Though being honest most of the stories were bad. How Melvin, Joe Joe and Claude wasn't about shit. How Leroy didn't come home last night or the night before. How, how one of them women claimed to be having a baby by her man! Those stories, the last ones especially, were shared with a sense of one uppence. Almost bragging rights as if to say even with all this on me "Still I rise". And they did.

In the middle of all of this were the jokes. The laughter, big belly laughs, the worse the problem the louder the laugh, the bigger the problems, the longer the laugh. And oh my the giggles, seeing those tired women giggle did something in my soul. Made me want to fetch more, bring more, turn more. Some mornings all they did was laugh and crack jokes. Left the stories about the kids, work, other women and their men on the front porch, to be picked up on their exit. Instead they told stories about their younger days before kids, before jobs and even before men though the men were always there even if they were boys. Told stories of how they sashayed here and there being young, how life was different back then. So very different back then.

I didn't realize then, that the laughs, the giggles, the jokes and even the sitting around the table was their armor. Put on piece by piece as they sat there knowing that when they rose, the world was still there; them bad ass kids, that damn job and those old worthless men. The battle to survive still had to be fought. Wasn't no getting sick or calling it quits on the mothering job, girlfriend job or the rare wife job. Too many depended on them, especially them kids, them bad ass kids. They were all waiting on her. That job that she was glad she had and that man, that man of hers who loved her but didn't love himself.

They would get up slowly, lazily even from the table, armor adjusting to match the sway of their full hips and swinging breasts. On some Saturday's, my mother stopped their migration by brewing another pot of coffee but this only delayed the battle and eventually they all slowly, lazily even, walked to the door. Ready.

I miss my momma's friends. Ms. Lovie, Ms Betty and the ones whose names don't easily come to mind but whose laughs I recall, as familiar to me as mine. I play them in my head, I play the soundtracks of their laughter when my armor is worn thin, rust spots showing. When glancing blows have a more lasting effect, I play them loudly while I drink my coffee, slowly as it cools before getting up, slowly, lazily even and walk toward the door, hips swaying and breasts swinging.

I got things to do, a battle to be won. Ready.

sistagirl

i call her my sistagirl
and she answers

sistagirl?!

yes?
what you want?
you know I'm busy…

i don't want
nothing
keep doing
what you doing

sistagirl?!

girl!
what you want
this time?!

nothing
juss wanted
to let you know
that i
love you

girl,
I know that
aint no surprise there
and
I love me

Anondra Williams

some you girl
now
I hope
you know that!

yeah sistagirl
I know you love me..

i call her my
sistagirl
and
she
answers

Once a Week

Once a week we go to bed early. Once a week we cut off the lights, silence the television and power down the laptops. Once a week we put the cat in the dog's bed and the dog, she takes a corner of our bed. Once a week we slide between cooled sheets and warmed comforters in a darkened bedroom high- lighted by outside flood lights. Two women, precautions.

We slide in with no expectations, naked sometimes literally and figuratively. She lays her head on my right breast, breath warming my skin. She talks, I listen. Slow rumbles about life, her long work days, how her boss is "special" and her assistant is to. How the cat bit her and the dog licked her when she came home. She loves the dog, tolerates the cat, her cat.

She talks about her dreams for her, for us, for the present and the future. She talks about her memories, stories about her church, pink bikes and next-door-neighbor crushes on girls when it should have been boys.

She talks and I listen, listen to her rumbles slow down, her smiles fade and her teeth, which I felt every time she laughed and smiled hard, become covered by lips. Lips I've touched briefly thought out the night in compliance with her requests for kisses and lip touches over shared laughter, anger and completion of various stories of I did, they did and I shoulda, woulda, coulda's.

She falls asleep, one night a week, in the dark, highlighted by flood lights and me. My warmth surrounding her, she sleeps better that way. My smell seeping into her skin til it seems as if we bathed with the same soap. We didn't, never do. I like scent, she prefers clean and clear.

I fall asleep eventually comforted by the weight of her, the sharing with her. We sleep like this til one of us decides to turn over or reach for that drink of water or that trip to the bathroom or even a cooler spot on the pillow. We do this once a week. Next week is my time. Next week we will cut off the lights, silence the television and power down the laptops. Next week we will put the cat in the dog's bed and the dog, she will take a corner of our bed. Next week we will slid between cooled sheets and warmed comforters in a darkened bedroom high- lighted by outside flood lights. Two women, precautions. I'll talk, she'll listen.

Life

We are living it. Doing the day to day stuff that makes up life. We meaning her and I or is it she and she because we are two women. Makes things more interesting, viewing everything from a feminine perspective that is. We've been doing this now for a little over a year. New for me, she on the other hand is a seasoned pro. Life happens when it's ready and not a minute before. But like I said we've been doing this for a little over a year now. Surprised me, honestly, that we have lasted this long. I ain't gonna lie it's because of her. From the beginning she's been the one pushing for me, for us.

Not to say that I've been fighting or even pushing back. I just, I just…I don't know, hell just figuring out who I am. Like I said I'm new to this. This woman loving woman thing, she's teaching me, I'm learning, being taught, accepting the difference.

And man are there differences. People talk about the obvious things, you know your family and friends disapproving. I expected that! Hell, I'm not slow, everything ain't for everybody. My family was all right. Granny and my momma stood by me. Couple of cousins, aunts and uncles fell to the wayside. No big loss, fair weather friends and family never are.

My job was cool as well. I took her to the company Christmas party with no issues at all. Doesn't hurt that she's beautiful, not in a model kind of way. More of a damn I bet she can cook, take care of home and good in bed as well way. And she was all that and much more, smart, compassionate and loving. She's teaching me that, the love part. Giving and receiving, who knew it wasn't natural. I thought I had been loving, turns out not so much.

So, like I said, I'm learning. I'm learning the things people don't talk about, especially the emotions involved in loving another woman. Everything is tripled! I mean everything and then you add in the additional conversations that happen between two women and damn. I mean seriously I think she talked me into this relationship, backed me into a corner with words and words and more words till finally I said yes, jus so the talking would stop.

No one mentioned the synching of our monthly periods or the hormonal craziness that stalks our home the second week of every month. I never got cramps before her, now every damn month I'm popping ibuprofen like an addict. She got my longer full-week cycle. Is this supposed to be considered an even trade?

I'm dealing with the emotions, the extra talking to get to a decision, the periods, society dealing with it all. Loving it. Yeah, I'm loving the hell out of her, us, even me. This woman loving woman thing.

BIG BLOCK LETTERS

BIG BLOCK LETTERS
TATTED ON PAPER

BIG BLOCK LETTERS
COMING THROUGHT TEXT MESSAGES
OF

HOW ARE YOU
DO YOU NEED SOMETHING
ARE YOU HUNGRY?
COLD?
MISSING ME?
I'M ON MY WAY HOME
….TO YOU

BIG BLOCK LETTERS
SHE TELLS ME
SHE LOVES
ME

BIG BLOCK LETTERS
AS SHE INTRODUCES ME
TO THEM ALL

THIS IS MY PARTNER
MAMA THIS IS THE ONE
YO, THAT'S MY LADY

BIG BLOCK LETTERS
SHE WRITES ON BOXES
KITCHEN, BEDROOM

AS SHE MOVES ME
TO HER

BIG BLOCK LETTERS
SHE PAINTS ON
THE WALL OF OUR
FIRST BORN
LOVE…

Letters followed over the years
GROWTH
CHANGE
She did
I did

LETTERS OF LIVING LIFE
ON BLACK STREETS IN
BROWN BUILDINGS
SURROUNDED BY
GREEN GRASS

SO WE GREW TOGETHER
TIL WE STOPPED
GROWING TOGETHER

little letters
no longer blocked
as we grew
and the kids grew

little letters sprinkled
casually, randomly
till they became

BIG BLOCK LETTERS
for her

DENIED IN THE BEGINNING
FRIENDSHIP ONLY
MENTIONED

BIG BLOCK LETTERS OF
LAUGHTER AND SHARING

BIG BLOCK LETTERS
COMING THROUGH TEXT MESSAGES
OF

HOW ARE YOU
DO YOU NEED ANYTHING
ARE YOU HUNGRY
COLD?
MISS ME?
I'M ON MY WAY HOME
…TO YOU

BIG BLOCK LETTERS
I LOVE YOU

She cooks for me...

She cooks for me
Southern style
as if
I'm starving
and this will be the last one
the last meal
the last love
every...time

She cooks
chicken
because all
of us love chicken
and peas
and cornbread
instead of french bread
because she just
doesn't get it
french bread that is
and besides cornbread
tastes better she says
I agree

She cooks for me
because she
says
she
loves
me
more than I
love

me

And I believe
her when she offers
me the first bite
followed by the last bite
followed by the
first sip
of ice tea, sweet
followed by the
last sip
of ice tea, sweet
because she loves me
southern style

Showing me love from
home
her momma and granny's front porch
how they showed love
with a hug
and a dish
of girl
you hungry?
come get you some
love..

She cooks for me
because feeding
me feeds her
she says
and every bite
I take
she swallows

Anondra Williams

Because
she loves me
Southern style

She cooks for me

Southern Loving

She calls me darling when she wants to cuddle, generally on a rainy, cloudy Saturday when the temperatures drop down below 60° but above 40°. She calls that cold and can't understand why I, a northern girl from Michigan, can still wear shorts on days like that. She also doesn't understand why I think that the heavy sweats and wool socks she sports on those days are funny. I have to explain that no, the heat will not be placed on eighty in the middle of the day, until the temperatures drop below zero. That hasn't happened yet so she accepts the blanket I toss her way along with grabbing me as another extra blanket.

The Mississippi in her comes out when she kisses me in the middle of cuddling, in the middle of our couch. All slow and lazy like she nibbles on my lips, talking in between sips of me. She giggles in her slightly deep husky drawl while telling me how much she loves her Northern girl, shorts and all. And she tells me that since she's cold, and I'm not, that I have to warm her up, from the inside out, as she takes me in, nibbles.

I oblige and rub her feet first, socks and all because she refuses to take them off "in the dead of winter." Slowly moving upwards, concentrating on her legs and thighs, circles of warmth. I touch her belly while she tells me stories of growing up under the hot yellow southern sun and we dream, seeds.

She tells me she doesn't understand why I can't eat cornbread and peas at every meal and asks how I could possibly choose potatoes over rice, a southern staple. It's like mother's milk, necessary to growth. That's my southern girl. She equates love to food and says quite often that food is love so she cooks, she feeds, she eats. My woman is a big girl, Mississippi thick girl. I had to learn that there is a difference. She pointed it out to me on the streets of our mid-size southern town. That right there is thick and that…that baby, baby girl, that right there is Mississippi thick. I saw. I got it. My girl, she's a Mississippi thick girl.

We live in a town that still rolls up some of its sidewalks at night, depending on what part of town you live in. A town where the neighbors know your name and they don't hesitate to use it, often, in passing and otherwise, depending on what side of town you live on.

I was scared, lesbian scared at first about living in the middle of red dirt, surrounded by red hate but my southern girl tried to grow outside of the red dirt of the south and couldn't. She became wilted in the hazy sun, missing her hot yellow, reds and greens even her blacks and whites. Recognized boundaries of what's not right but accepted, she was use to.

She met me though, in the brown fields and lakes of the north and convinced me that her and red dirt and grits would be all I need to grow, to be more than I was. So here we are five years later, me and my southern girl. Firmly planted and replanted, sprouting in this fertile red dirt telling warm stories on cold days to remember choices made.

She cooks me grits every Sunday morning. Sometimes she even brings them to me in bed when she thinks I deserve it, when my northern sensibilities have blended well with her southern common sense and charm. Carrying them in and waking me with the smell of them in a red bowl, bacon and eggs on a separate plate because I don't like my food to touch as she says "baby, baby girl, wake up it's time for some love."

I love my southern girl and our southern loving.

Remember

Thinking
On you
Mentally rambling
On you

And what we did
Or do
Depending on whose asking

Date and time
Variables
Of fucking

Yeah fucking
Cause making love came after

Remember?

Times spent slowly licking
Drips and drops
No touching please
With fingers and hands
And hanging body parts
Real or imagined

Filling sinks and crevasses
With you
And me
Turns

Slow torture

Painful pleasure
You gave
I sought
Shelter in us

Remember?

Discovering salty and sweet
Not limited to food
And dining…
tables

corners and curves
dark passageways
long and short
covered
by scents
masquerading as fruit and flowers
trails of you
I sought..

And you gave

Remember?

Sweating and bumping
And grinding
Seeking…
That ultimate

That only you could give me

While wrapped between thighs

And arms, legs attempting
Hands clenching, reaching
Lips..
Spasms
In we of course
I was giving
And we were taking
Turns

Again

Remember?

Sweet Tea...

I love me some sweet tea, a glassful of ice cubes covered in brown real sugar sweetness. I swear each bead of moisture along the sides of the glass calls my name, teasing me with the coldness inside, the sugar, the flavor of the crisp tea inside. Each bead screaming at me that the inside is going to be all that as it slides across my teeth and tongue and down my throat, to rest in my belly. Cooling me off slowly from the inside out, cool tendrils escaping to all parts of me, tips of fingers and toes...knee caps and elbows even. I love me some sweet tea.

She, my love, has a cold glass ready for me every day when I get in from work. Not because she has to, but because she wants to. Her way of welcoming me home from a day of not being around her. I appreciate it, anticipate it, expect it...need it. Her lips, the sweet tea, her arms wrapping around me, the sweet tea sliding down me, her hands curving to the small of my back as she holds me as I drink the sweet tea slowly.

They are almost one and the same, sweet tea and her; I love them both.

Something about sweet tea always reminds me of my childhood, granny and momma and them and now her. Every sip I savor, eyes closed, holding the glass up to my lips as the last drop passes through and the ice rests on the outside of my lips coating them with the remnants of sweat tea, fills me with love and laughter, good time memories. She waits until I finish, til my throat relaxes and my eyes open before taking the glass from my hand and licking the sweet tea slowly off my lips. Not missing a drop, taking moisture and replacing it at the same time she encircles me with her tongue and lips and occasionally teeth, getting all of the sweet teal while leaving her behind.

I love me some sweet tea; I love me some her.

She is my tea, before a little water is added, before the sugar, and well before the lemons that some tease the tea with. She is the plucked tea leaf before it's dried, rich in smell and texture. I rub her in between my fingers, like loose tea leaves, smelling the richness of her slowly seeping upward, nose buried deep, debating on green or black. She doesn't mind that I consider her taste to be bitter sweet at times, she knows that tea, sweet tea and her, I love. Variety, herbal and otherwise.

I asked her once why she always licks the tea off my lips and she said because it tasted sweeter, richer, better after being tasted by me. I understood.

I love me some sweet tea, I love me some her.

Years

Simple shit…

I swear she be on the simplest of shit, always talking about simple stuff like love and lifelong relationships to taking care of me. I hear her, but I'm not feeling her like that. I'm only thirty, and that forever shit is for chicks over forty or at least thirty-five. I told her to check back then and until then I'm partying and fucking at the same damn time.

Simple shit

I swear she be on the simplest of shit. Always talking simple stuff about clubbing , hanging out and fucking. I hear her but I'm feeling more than that. Sure I could just fuck her and keep it moving but I see so much in her beyond a simple fuck. I see my future, our future entwined. Besides I'm past the club scene, that's for your young chicks. She told me to check back in five years. Ain't that some shit.

One year

One year later and she still popping up talking about love and forever. I told her nothing has changed and I'm not ready. She thinks pointing out how my life is a series of nothing but partying and random, one-night stands is a bad thing. I told her it's what I want.

Shit I know I got issues. I know I should be past this but I'm not and no amount of preaching is going to change that. She says I'm scared to love, scared to love her. She might be right. Love has never been a part of me from birth. I don't think my mom loved me. She had me, fed me, clothed me and sheltered me, but that's about it. I've tried to explain this to her. All she responds with is she can teach me how to love her. She's not hearing me when I say I don't want to learn.

One year…

I'm still trying to convince her of the love we can have, the love I'm offering. I understand not understanding love. It hasn't always been a part of my life either but she doesn't want to hear that. She rather keep crying the same ol song of "love don't live here anymore" and it never did.

Two years…

I know she's a good woman. She proves it daily, has proven it the last two years. Last winter I had the flu, she was the only one who checked on me, even made me soup. She wanted to stay over but I didn't want to pass on my germs. Didn't work; she ended up with the flu anyway. I didn't check on her, didn't want to get sick again. She said she understood. Plenty of other folks stopped by, I heard them in the background the one time I called.

Maybe they were offering the love she wants. Yeah I know that sounds shitty but hey I never said I was a nice person. If you ask her I never say anything nice at all. I told her she gives good head, for some reason that really pissed her off.

I think a part of her is mad that every now and then she succumbs to my womanly wiles and sleeps with me. Mentally attempting to discount all that have went before her and those who will follow after her. At least I'm honest about what I do.

I know I'm not the only one she's spewing this forever love shit to. I can't be, just isn't logical. Like I said she's a good woman. Just not the woman for me right now.

Two years…

I'm trying, lord knows I am. Can you believe she didn't even bother to come check on me when I had the flu? Hell I got it from her. Thank goodness my momma and them came over every day to care for me. My granny even stayed over one night.

A friend stayed over as well. She brought me soup, a couple of movies and company. Good company. Though it wasn't the company of the person I wanted. She said she wasn't offering anything but friendship. I accepted too quickly the company that came after as well. Accepted too quickly the surprise dinners and random I'm thinking of you texts. I accepted the sex. Yes, the sex. The hugs, kisses and touches I was craving from her, from her. I looked up from a kiss and six months had passed. Six months of receiving love from her and silence from her. I debated on reaching out to her. I mean life was good with her and obviously things weren't changing with HER. I'm sure she's still clubbing and fucking.

I sent a text. She responded.

Three years…

She got a girl now. Doesn't surprise me, seeing as how she's so eager to love. Doesn't hurt. Not one bit. I knew she would leave me along eventually. She still pops up every month or so, random texts asking how I'm doing or if I need something. Every now and then she tells me she loves me, still loves me.

I wonder if her girl knows about me. I'm tempted to ask but I'm not messy, besides I don't want her. At least not now, she got a girl.

Three years…

I love her. I love Her.

Four years..

I stopped clubbing a few months ago, trying to get further at my job or should I say career. Clubbing every night and trying to make it in and function by 9am just wasn't happening any more. I'm getting old, the scene was getting old and the chicks were getting younger. Always wanting to fight and shit. I ain't got time for that.

I stopped sleeping around as much, had a scare. Thought that one chick had burnt me with the gift that keeps on giving turns out it was just a fever blister. After her all of them looked like they were walking around with something. One girl even told me that everyone got something so it shouldn't matter. Yeah, she had to go after that comment.

We haven't been talking as much lately, texts and calls becoming less frequent. I see her and her girl around every now and then. She pretends she doesn't see me but I always get a text soon after. I'm cool with that. I understand, life goes on. I knew she wouldn't stick around forever. She hasn't said she loves me in awhile. Doesn't hurt.

Four years…

I'm trying to work with her because she loves me and I love her. Almost two years and we've been doing all right. I'm happy, she's happy.

I see Her around every now and then, she still looks the same…beautiful. I don't text or call as much because I'm trying with her, she loves me and I, I love her.

Five years…

I sent her a text, told her today makes five years. Don't get me wrong, I sat and thought about sending her that but I'm ready..finally. What happens, happens. I told her to wait on me.

Five years..

And she sends me a text, telling me today is the day. I read that text over and over for hours, trying to decipher what it meant. Read it while eating dinner with her at our kitchen table. Read it while sitting next to her on our couch in our home. Laid down that night, with the words embedded in my head, tatted on the inside of my lids. It's been five years. Five years of waiting, dealing with her being her. Doing what she does and who she does. Two years of me loving and living with her. I promised her things as well.

Text sent back...

I'm on my way.

Trying

We trying
to be more than
what we are
while thinking
love don't make it
right

her version of
events
ain't the same story
I'm living and sharing

but we trying to see
the other's point
of view
while seeing
that
maybe we
jumped too soon
believed to easily
that we
we would be different

instant attraction
add water
stir
in the middle of
instant love
bake at 350

we trying

day in, day out
night passes
and we still

not talking
about the elephant
in the room
while playing
with dogs and cats

oh and we
ain't fucking
cause the attraction
that was so strong
when long distance
was a factor
and big dreams
were a factor
and when secret weekends
were a factor
ain't there
no more

explained away
by work
and stress
and living
and stress

with side eyes
of I thought
you were
better than this

different than them
but I see
you not

we trying
to accept
reality

Lost

I am amazed by women
and their desire to
be involved
with involved
not in love
with love
but in love
with not being alone

Crying tears of stress
on Saturday
climaxing
on Sunday
to random text message alerts
saying nothing
but sending hope
like smoke signals
from the Indians...
they still lost

New Pussy

I was young when I met her, young in mind, body and spirit. In this instance two out of three is a bad thing. I was twenty-one and thought I knew everything there was to know about life, love and living it to the fullest.

I had been on my own since I was 18, thrown out when my mother figured out I was a bull dagging dyke. Told me to take my dyking ass out her house and life. I knew the day was coming and was sort of prepared. I had been slowly moving clothes and personal stuff for months to a friends spot because I knew my momma. Wasn't nothing that wasn't the lords way, going on in her house.

My momma was living proof that a reformed hoe made the best Christian. When the rumors finally got to her saved, sanctified and filled with the holy ghost ears, she confronted me. Bible in hand and preacher in tow. She was sleeping with him even then, but hey who am I to judge. The confirmation was sort of anti-climatic in my eyes.

Momma- "Is you a bulldagger, one of them lezbeens?"

Me- "Yes, ma'am."

Momma- "You gonna have to get on out of

here with that. I'm not going to have that evilness around my other children." This was said as she clutched the bible tighter and the preachers eyes got bigger. He hadn't said a word so far, I think he was picturing me and other women together. His own personal Sodom and Gomorrah and not in a good way.

Me- "Yes, ma'am. I'll be out by tomorrow."

And I was, haven't been back since. I see my brothers and sisters though. They tell me momma and the preacher man got a thing going on and that momma don't go to church as much since his wife found out. Again, who am I to judge.

Like I was saying I met her at twenty-one. I thought I was ready for a real relationship. Told all my road dawgs and hanging partners I was going to settle down, that I was looking for the one, my queen, my wifey.

Yes, I used the word wifey. I told you I was young. After putting it out in the Universe, I found her. That's right within six months I found her. She was love and light and all my missing parts. Slightly older, she was looking to be a wife.

So we did it, moved in after dating less than six months. Yea, I know way too soon but we wanted the same thing, moving quickly wasn't an issue. And nothing was an issue for over ten years. That's right ten long years. For ten long years we did the damn thing. Woke up every day together, went to bed every night together and all the togetherness we could stomach in between.

The newness quickly wore off but the comfort didn't, it grew. We grew, slowly and steadily. We also became "that couple," the couple that everyone wanted to be. The couple everyone thought would be together forever. As my granny use to say, "Forever is a mighty long time" and it turns out I wasn't built for forever at least not with her.

After many mornings of waking up just because that's what you are supposed to do I decided it was time for a change. Or maybe I decided I wanted more or possibly less. More or less I was done. To say she was surprised would be an understatement and this time it was climatic to say the least.

"I don't want this anymore."

"Want what anymore?"

"This, this relationship. Us, this home, this life. I want to be free."

That started hours and hours of tears, crying,

begging and pleading. I was firm though, I just didn't want this anymore. Didn't want to wake up to her, go to sleep with her. Growing wasn't something we were doing or at least I wasn't. I watched this strong woman that loved me, loved us become reduced to a wet and sniffling mess over the next few days. Saw her strength fade and mine grow. I grew from each tear, each sob, each question asked why. I was brutally honest with her, to honest looking back. There wasn't no reason to hurt her like I did.

That rash and brash twenty-one year old was still there and she popped up with the quickness ready to speak for me anytime I thought about wavering. She told me about all the new pussy that we could have, all the clubs we could party in, all the late night fun in different cities. My dawgs were happy for me, wanted me to come out and play in the streets with them. You know like puppies do and shit. Made sense to me then. New pussy, new parties, new memories and all without her.

It worked out for a hot Mississippi minute, new pussy, even some of the ones that knew me when we were a couple, lots of them came out of the woodwork to show me a good time, explain to me what I had been missing. I turned down her best friend. I couldn't stoop that low, though I did tell her to watch them wolves around her. She didn't respond to my text. I understood.

She hadn't responded to anything I sent her in the twelve months since I moved out. Not one word. It was like I didn't exist to her anymore. I sent her emails, you know checking up on her. Nothing. Sent her messages via Facebook till she blocked me. I even mailed her an old fashioned handwritten letter. Nothing. I dropped by the house one day but she wasn't there and none of our old stuff was there, new folks answered the door, said they bought the house three months ago. I didn't get a penny of that money. Not that I'm complaining but damn I did put six years into that home, made them monthly mortgage payments with her and shit.

Here I sit waiting on slow ass new pussy to come over so I can take her slow ass out to eat on my dime. I don't really even like her all that much but it's something to do. My homeys all got girls and they can't kick it but maybe once every other month. That partying all night in new cities lasted for maybe a month. The ones who are single, are bitter and mad about it. I can't blame them the chicks out here today don't want to work for nothing, have nothing. They not trying to build or grow. Grow like we did. Grow like I thought I did, was but wasn't if I had I wouldn't be here.

I sent her my last text last night… "I'm

sorry." She didn't respond, I understand. New pussy did though asking what I was going to buy her. Shit.

Swimming

On our first date she had two drinks. I didn't really notice til later, much later, reminiscing on things. She had a drink during dinner, another after dinner over conversation. Normal. Our fourth date, on a Saturday, she had to cancel. She said something came up. I couldn't really understand her, due to the slurring of her voice. I was concerned and asked if she was sick. She wasn't. Recovery, explained later, much later.

By our sixth date I noticed that the two drinks was now several, with quite a few happening before our date. I questioned her on the tenth date. Only because the car was swerving and so was she. I only questioned the amount for that night. Not the other nights or days. Decisions. Choices.

Her response was to apologize and to promise not to drink and drive again. I accepted. I accepted becoming her designated driver. It made sense. I didn't drink much, never cared for the taste of alcohol. Nor the effects. She enjoyed it, and besides it wasn't every day, only on the weekends. I was happy that she felt comfortable enough around me to be herself.

The first time she passed out I was glad I was there. Things can happen to women who pass out in clubs. As it was I could barely get help to get her to the car. The guy who did, he didn't hold her right and her head hit the door frame of the building and the car. I was surprised. She didn't wake up once. She didn't waken once we arrived at her home either, well not enough to be useful. I was tempted to leave her in the car but that would have been wrong. It wasn't her fault that the bartender made the drinks too strong. We discussed it the next day, after the headache went away for her and the sleepless night on the couch for me, and decided to never go to that club again.

That was the first of many clubs and bars we were never to frequent again over the years for various reasons, eventually we just stayed at home. It was easier for her and me, easier for her to pass out on the couch, easier for me to listen to her drunken insults in private versus public. Yea she was a mean drunk, found that out after we moved in together.

Don't get me wrong she has never hit me, really didn't need to. I was beaten down before I ever met her. Allowed too much way too many years ago. I recognized but didn't acknowledge the signs. My father was a drunk and my mother let him be a drunk. At least he was a functioning one, up to his death, he worked Monday through Friday. He died on a Saturday. She, she doesn't function anymore, at least not in a recognizable way to society. My mother doesn't like her.

At first she was only drunk on the weekends, starting on Friday afternoons after work and recovering on Sunday afternoon, to prepare for work. Sunday soon started slipping away from her and recovering started happening on Monday's. Mondays turned into Tuesday's, never made it to Wednesday. They fired her.

I understood and believed her that it was because she was a black lesbian, not the thirty five days she didn't make it in on Monday, the twenty five days she didn't make it on Tuesday. I believed her when she said they were scared and jealous of a black lesbian. I believed her when she got fired at the seven jobs after that. I believed her when she said she was looking for a new one every day and that she was going to the interviews she was told me she was getting. That was two years ago. I stopped asking about them. You know there's a recession going on and I make just enough to cover the bills, so I do.

And I do love her which is why I don't hesitate to support her. I understand that she's doing all she can. I got her to attend the classes and support groups, had a sponsor. They didn't get her like I do. They told her to just stop. I told her to slow down. Sometimes she listens.

Either way I have to stop by the liquor store
on my way home, she says the pool is dry.
Swimming.

Let's talk

We don't do that no more
Mainly we…
Let's fuck
We don't do that no more
Mainly we…
Let's fight
And then make up so
We can
Fuck
Let's talk
About fucking
Cause fucking is on my mind
And I wanna do
What we talking about
Fuck
I'm getting excited
About
Fucking

I'm listening…

bored

Last night we fucked. Seriously. We fucked. No foreplay, mental or otherwise. Just fucking, licking and grinding. Not all night, but long enough. She came first. She came again. I'm easy, I came. We went to bed early, intentions of falling asleep. I was tired, she was bored. Not the best combination. Maybe.

I sleep in the nude, she doesn't. I'm easy. When I felt her hand sliding across my right thigh as I was drifting on the verge of sleep, I was surprised. Thought for a second she was hand-walking in her sleep. I thought that till her hand kept moving, till she touched my pussy. Kept thinking that even when her middle finger separated my lips and slid into my pussy, up till her knuckle. No more hand-walking. We driving.

It slid in easily, so did the other two as I rode her hand, as she whispered in my ear how wet and warm I was. She licked my lobe and told me how easy it was to fuck me, how my legs just opened up and my pussy jumped on her fingers.

I was mute as my body tried to take what she was offering, tugging and pulling those fingers inside me, slamming down onto the top of her palm, squeezing all of me onto her. Did I mention she came first? While she was fucking me, she was touching herself, getting off on my warmth and wetness while I got off on her firmness, thick. She's bilingual, trilingual or whatever shit. Who cares? She was touching herself and me at the same damn time. Picture that.

She came before me. She does know herself best, I wasn't complaining as I continued to ride her hand. Cuming, finally. It wasn't a pretty climax either but damn it was good, my body shook and throbbed, pulsed. She likes the feeling of my body humming on her hand.

I finally un-muted myself to ask her where that came from. She responded by tugging off her t-shirt and climbing on top of my face. That was my answer.

The wet musky smell of her hit me before the semi-sweet taste of her coated my tongue, my lips, my nose and my chin. She talks a lot of shit when she's getting fucked, or fucking. I didn't mind. I'm easy. I let my tongue talk back to her as I rode her clit sidesaddle. I gripped her hips with both hands to keep her in place, wasn't easy. She was bucking as I licked, suck and sometimes bit anything in the vicinity of my mouth. There was a lot, even more as she ground against my mouth, giving me all of her as she came, quicker than expected. Juices. Slick. Heat. More cum than expected as I drank and drank.

She apologized as she looked down at me through her titties, looked down at her pussy sitting on my face. Apologized for making me drink all of her, take all of her. Apologized for fucking my face so hard, there would be bruises tomorrow. Apologized as she squeezed her thighs around my face and told me, she needed more, had more to give. I obliged. I'm easy.

She rode me again, my face, slower this time. No urgency. Not on her part as I was surrounded by heat, thigh heat, pussy heat...body heat. Up and down, she rode my tongue, in and out. I was her tool, her rabbit, her personal bullet. The one she called girlfriend. She came, thicker, dryer this time. Deeper though as she whispered my name through the lips of her pussy, teaching me how to really pronounce it.

Finally she slid off of me, letting me have a drink of cool air. She asked if I wanted a towel to wipe up her juices or a cup of water to wash down the juices. I declined. Told her I was tired and had every intention of falling asleep with her juices on me and in me. She smiled and kissed my lips, laying her cheek on my still sticky face while inhaling deeply and saying "I'm sleepy to. We should go to bed early more often. Night baby."

I agreed. I'm easy. Besides, tomorrow night I might be the one bored.

Promises

she promised me
the sun, the moon and
the stars
all between her thighs

I believed her
as she spread
them wide
for my viewing
pleasure

I gazed in wonder
disbelief
when I realized
her pussy
looked like
all the rest

smelled like all
the others
when clean
tasted slightly sweeter
but who wants
sweet pussy?

I mean I don't
want it bitter
but I don't want it
like sugar either

and maybe I'm not

the typical lesbian
who thinks that
pussy rules
everything around me

it's all right

the reality
of the situation
is that pussy
is an inanimate object
controlled by
the mind, heart
and possibly them thighs

so had she promised
me the sun, the moon
and the stars
while opening
up her mind, heart
and yes, them thighs
maybe...maybe
we would be together
and this poem
wouldn't be the period
on our relationship
as I asked her
politely
please
ms
close them thighs
there are adults present

Firsts

I saw her first in 6th grade. I ignored her because she was acting like one of them, a knuckle-headed boy. She was always running around with her clothes half off, boy clothes at that and a basketball in her hands. She ignored me as well. Not that I noticed. I mean she was a girl who acted like a boy, totally beneath me.

I saw her again in the 11th grade. I mean I had seen her before but, you know she was just there, part of the scenery. This day she stood out. Still dressing like a boy, but it fit now, the clothes and the look. The basketball wasn't too far away. It fit as well; it fit her 6ft frame slim frame. She smiled a lot. I noticed that. Never at me, not that I really noticed but others were always talking about her teeth and lips, tongue to if the rumors were to be believed. I didn't listen. Not really what I was interested in.

We started to speak, at least when spoken to in the crowded hallways between classes. She was with hers and I was with mine. Girlfriend and boyfriend that is, I had one and she had the other. They were in love, high school love, grade school love even. They had been together since then. Me, I played around a little bit more. Liked to show my teeth to every pretty girl I met as my grandma used to say. I was the talk of the school, ol pretty girl who liked them other pretty girls and wasn't afraid to let everyone and her mama know.

This day I stopped, paused as high school life went around me. Made her pause, stop, waiting on me. I said the obvious.

"Good game", teeth showing.

She flashed hers in return, "Thanks."

And that was that. I moved on, she moved on. I didn't look back. She wasn't ready.

I saw her again in college, Sophomore year. She was a basketball star and I, I was a star with the ladies. I went to school to school ladies, be they fem, stud or anything in between. She was still claiming straight but I could see the real her trying to burst out. She and he had finally broken up, freshman year of college. Someone said she wasn't giving it up. I didn't believe that.

This day I stopped, paused as college life moved around me. Made her pause, stop, waiting on me.

"Why don't you smile at me a little bit more?" I asked with the utmost sincerity that a 20 year old who thinks the moon rises and sets on her left and right ass cheeks could muster. I think I threw her for a loop. Maybe she was expecting more of the "good game" from before. We were past that, she was ready.

She half smiled and said "How's that? Will that do?"

"For now, sure but later I expect more"

"More? Later?"

"Yeah, I'll come scoop you around 8 tonight. I got the feeling you need to get off this campus and I know I do."

"I do need to get off but why would I go with you?" she asked with a puzzled expression across her strong brow. Never noticed really how thick her eyebrows where, but they were. Fingertip thick.

"Because you are ready, now." I answered with teeth, lips and tongue showing.

"Ready for what?"

"For me."

"For you? I've know you since ever and a day. What more do I need to be ready for?"

"Meet me at 8 tonight and you will find out" and with that I walked away. Didn't look back, didn't need to. I knew she was looking, debating and in the end accepting.

She was ready at 8. Early even. We rode out to dinner at a local mom and pop Italian spot, off the beaten pathway of the typical college crowd. I like to take them out of the way, till they know their way. The way I roll. I know I sound sorta…whorish. But I promise it's not like that. I just know what I like, fortunately most like me as well. Stacked intelligent aggressive fem, what more do you need?

We talked over bread, pasta and candle light. Caught up on the obvious, connected friends from home, the questioning exchange of why we never hung out in high school. I let her talk, till they got ready to close the doors. Then I paid, took her hand and exited.

I didn't take her back to the dorms, like I said I needed a break from the college life and I knew she did. I could feel the tension all through dinner, expectation building as I let her ramble. She really didn't know what to expect. I liked that. I liked her. Had liked her for awhile, but like I said she wasn't ready. She wasn't ready to acknowledge that she liked women. Not like in "bestie" like. Like in, I want to taste you from head to toe and every place in between. She's probably not quite there yet but she's close enough for me to make my move, finally.

I've been watching her, watch others from the sidelines of the basketball court and life. Watching her deny the obvious every time the question is asked while hanging onto him, when he was doing other things and other bodies. I know her family, I understand.

She moved slowly from the parking lot of the local motel to the room I had gotten earlier. I smiled, teeth showing.

"Girl come on, you act like I'm going to eat you up or something. I'm not the big bad wolf and you are not Red Riding Hood…well, unless you like role play and if that's the case, I'll go back to the car and get my cape." I said with laughter in my voice, teeth showing even more as she came to a complete stop halfway.

"Look, I'm tired and maybe we should just go back to the dorms. If we don't make it back by midnight, you know they lock the doors now."

"Yeah, I know and that's why I got a room. I didn't feel like rushing back after our talk." I answered with a tug.

"Wait a minute, what talk?" she asked with

the sounds of frustration in her voice.

"The talk we are about to have." I answered with none in mine. I was happy inside, geeked about the future. Our future. She just didn't know it yet.

"Hold up, we just spent the last three hours talking, what more do we have to talk about." She stood her ground. All 6ft standing stiff in the cold night air, locs flowing slightly.

"About me and you. Now come on. I'm not one for standing outside and letting the birdies chirp my business in the streets." I tugged her hand again, pulling her along while noticing the nails and length of her fingers. She has big hands.

I taught her how to use those hands, those fingers over the next few months, years. It wasn't easy let me tell ya. Yes, she went in the room that night finally. Sat on that bed scared, almost as if she expected her momma and them to come bum rushing out of the bathroom with crosses, holy water and bible scriptures. Honestly her fear and their actions wasn't probably too much from the truth, them southern Baptists ain't not joke.

She sat and listened to me tell her she was meant to be mine. I listened to her tell me she was straight, loved men and I was crazy, listened as I kissed away the denial and kissed in her acceptance. Oh don't get me wrong we didn't go past a lot of more talking and some scattered kissing that night. Reality of it was it took a few months of her going back and forth between me and a few others before she finally accepted her truth. Our truth. I was her first though, first real love, first time being her. Everything don't come easy to everyone, I knew that.

I look at her now, two years later all confident with who she is, where she going and how she's going to get there. I'm right there by her side. I came to school to school women, did that, had my fun, she's my life. She's my first also, first love. Real.

15

That's how long we've been together. 15 years, 15 long years. 15 years of ups and downs and a lot of in betweens. If you had asked us 15 years ago when we met randomly at one of those black women empowerment functions that was secretly a spot for single women to meet and greet while pretending they down for the cause. Hey I'm not knocking it, just telling the truth as I know it.

I'm sure there were women there who were there to uplift and support and grow. Me, I was there to meet a closeted lesbian or bi-sexual chick who wouldn't mind a one night stand. I was not there to fall in love or anything near it. As the old song goes "Love don't live here anymore".

I was over 30 when I realized women weren't about shit. Sorry, just my truth. Unfortunately I still wanted to have sex with said women, be they shit worthy or not. I found a solution at these types of meetings. There was always a closeted chick who didn't want anyone to know and who couldn't put up much of a fuss when you didn't return their calls after a few wild nights. The threat of outing quickly killed the fuss of those who tried to complain.

So like I said I was trolling for some random strange after the meeting was over and I was sending signals to this one chick who had been staring and licking her lips all night. I was thinking on a quick dine and dash because she wasn't really my type in the daylight but would do for one night, no more and possibly less.

When she bumped into me, on purpose or not, she apologized and kept it moving. I would love to say our eyes met and my fate was sealed but that would be a lie, a pretty one but still a lie. Matter of fact she barely looked at me. I recognized her as the sista who was co-leading the meeting, striking, beautiful, captivating, and way out of my league or should I say not what I was currently looking for. She was one of them relationship type women, though I couldn't tell if she was gay or straight.

That question was answered a month later when I ran into her at a friend's BBQ. She was there with someone else and pretended not to recognize me at first. When I reminded her, the expression on her face wasn't pleasant or personable. A stank face would be the more apt description. That face lead to our first real conversation.

"Why the stank face?"

"Because you are sort of a stank person."

"Damn that's harsh and nasty."

"No more harsh and nasty than what I hear and see from you."

"Hold up, you don't even know me!" I exclaimed with an attitude to match her stank one.

"Girl everyone knows you and your trifling ways. Preying on closeted lesbians and bi-sexual women for a quick fuck, you ain't bout shit."

And with that she walked off leaving me standing in a pile of my own shit. It never occurred to me that the women I was messing around with where talking to other women. After picking my chin up off the grass, I left the party. I needed a quiet moment and place to process this new information and besides my couch was calling my name. Last night's random strange had tired a sista out.

Part of my processing was reaching out to various friends over the next few days and they all happily and gladly confirmed my well-earned reputation as someone who wasn't about shit. I was hurt by the glee in which the information was given and quickly realized that I didn't really have any friends, at least not the kind that would have told me long ago to cut the bullshit out and woman up. I'm not going to tell you that I changed overnight, I didn't. I did change though, mainly because of her and little bit because of me, hell it was time. It seemed like everywhere I went, she was there with that stank face, pissing on my parade. Eventually she had no choice and had to stop making them faces, I forced her to. Every time I saw her, I spoke, sometimes two or three times a night. I don't know why I did it, I mean outside of it pissing her off the first few times, after that she expected it and was ready with a fake greeting followed quickly by that stank face.

One day we had a real conversation beyond "hey, hey back insert fake face", we discussed the reason for the meeting and I added my two cents on some things I felt was lacking in her groups planning. Yes I was still coming to the meetings, though not for the reasons you thinking. Either way her reaction was funny, she did the slow blink, before nodding in slight agreement. She then went on to tell me the things she was working on to improve the mission and looking for people who were really truly dedicated. I know right about now you thinking, we held hands and ran through a field of purple flowers in love. We didn't. I don't like group stuff, so I didn't join but I did allow her to pick my brain and bounce ideas and suggestions off of me. That's really where it started. She figured out I wasn't a total asshole and I, well I just stopped being an asshole.

Finally I asked her out, casually in the

middle of her going on and on about some cause she was thinking on supporting. She slowed down enough to say yes and then, then we ran in a field of purple flowers holding hands. She skipped, I did more of a step-bounce. Just kidding, it took way way more than one date to convince her of a future with me. Yeah me convincing her, somewhere in the middle of one of those stank faces and brain picking conversations, I fell in love. She didn't, well not at first. I think she still saw the asshole shine through too much in the beginning to really see the hurt woman underneath. One day she did.

It was a slow courtship, lasted more than a year. In that year we spent a lot of time talking, sharing and healing. Turns out I wasn't the only one recovering from this war called love. She had been hurt, played and fucked over and this was one of the reasons why she was involved in saving every bird, frog and tree group in our area. It was her way of running and hiding. You join enough committees you won't notice that you haven't been on a date in two years, busy.

Two hurt women trying to love is a beautiful thing to see. It really is. We both tried so much to be better, to do better. It worked. After she really started believing in us, in me really. Asshole and all.

So here were are, 15 years later. I count the

first day we met as the start our 15 years, she
doesn't. Says we didn't really start for another year
and a half, maybe two years after meeting. I just let
her keep counting the way she wants and I keep
counting the way I want. Every now and then I
catch her staring at me out of the corner of her eye,
I think she's looking to see if that asshole she met
15 years ago is still lurking around. She's been
gone, 15 years gone.

Thirds

Everyone thinks it's all about sex. I wish it was that simple, not that sex between two willing adults is simple, add in a third and well shit gets interesting to say the least.

She joined us after we were together for three years. Something discussed during dating, the possibility of a third one day when we both wanted it. It was more than sex we wanted, we wanted an addition to our permanent family. She, me and her.

Even though we discussed it, dreamt it even, the reality was different, even the timing of her coming into our lives. We weren't going through a bad patch or even looking. We were living and loving as best as two women can and doing a damn good job of it. All while being honest with each other after past pretend relationships.

Dreams and reality shared over a table of living. We grew. We grew so much that I forgot about the possibility of an addition till we bumped into her. The club scene wasn't our thing but a house party was right up our alley. Something about grooving around a couch and a chair and using someone's guest towels made me smile deep inside. We were in the groove and in the corner of one of Z's friend's home surveying the slightly crowded room when she entered. Life didn't stop or anything like that but she did draw both of our attention. That in itself was odd since we liked things a little bit different from the other. I was the more fem of the two of us at least on the surface. The bedroom told a different story. It worked for us.

She saw her first, though I doubt more than thirty seconds before me. I stated the obvious first.

"Nice."

She agreed with a softly uttered "Very."

We watched as she slowly made her way through the room, stopping and chatting with a few, waving at others without approaching. There was no reason for her to stop by us, speak to either of us but she did. She did with a half smile and a slight eye-tilt.

"Hey"

I smiled back with all of my teeth. "Hey right back at you, I'm Z and you are?"

"Free, my mom was a free spirit when being free wasn't an option" she explained with a smaller smile before looking at my partner with a questioning gaze.

"Oh hi, I'm Nicole, nice to meet you." she responded with as many teeth as possible. I would have been jealous if I didn't understand the why. The "why" that was standing in front of us.

"Nice to meet you both. So tell me are you two uhmmm together? Couple together not hanging out together" she asked with a slight smile present.

It appeared I was taking the lead as always as I responded with "Yes."

The slight smile turned wistful as she stated, "It figures, the two women I'm attracted to would be attached to each other."

"Oh so you're attracted to both of us?" the girlfriend came out of her staring stupor to ask. I swear when we get home, she's going to get a spanking, whether she wants it or not.

"Yes."

"That's interesting and not necessarily a bad thing" I said while relaxing my pose to lean against the wall a little bit more, settling in as things became more and more interesting.

"Why not?" was the obvious question asked by her.

"We're open to you, the idea of you, the possibility of you." I answered

"So you want to fuck me, a threesome?"

"Yes". I waited a heartbeat or two before finishing with "That's not all of course. Our sex life is great, fantastic even. Adding you to it would be nice, but not necessary. We're looking, no that's not the right word. We're interested in a third."

"What's a third?"

"A third is our equal, our partner, the other person in our relationship."

"And you haven't been looking?"

"That's the interesting part, we haven't, figured she would appear when the time was right", I looked at Nicole to confirm.

"Z's right, we haven't been looking. It's one of those things we spoke on years ago as a possibility. You know groundwork when building a relationship. What you will and won't do type of stuff. And now here you are." Nicole stated the not so obvious while settling in next to me on the wall that was supporting not only us but possibly our future.

Hours passed on that wall as we all talked, flirted even and discussed the idea of thirds. Something never thought on by her. It was interesting to say the least. To see the sparks fly, the seeds being possibly planted.

Don't get me wrong we didn't leave the party and go fuck. Naw real life doesn't work like that, at least not in this relationship. We dated her, courted her, allowed her into our lives before sex became a necessity and not just a fun option. Six months after meeting we all went and took the "big" test together along with some smaller tests at the ob's office. Can't be too careful in this day and age. Everything that looks pretty isn't.

And like we both said, we really weren't looking. She wasn't either at least not for US. It took time to get to know her and vice versa. And let me tell you it wasn't always roses and sunshine. Nic and I were used to each other. Use to who was a morning person and who dealt with it. Who went through periods of I don't eat meat in public but please slip me a piece of your pork when no one is looking. Free had to get in where she fit in sometimes and we had to remember that she was there and her opinion not only mattered but counted.

That was two years ago, two years of trying to figure out where we are at for a while before accepting we are here, three same gender women loving and living under one roof, one bed. It works for us is what I tell folks when I introduce the loves of my life. It doesn't work for all even the ones who continually judge from the sidelines. Me, Free and Z are doing it, first, second and thirds.

Mind Fuck

We were talking. We had been talking for some hours. Rambling conversation of a get to know you and I just like the sound of your voice and the way you breathe in and out type conversations. She did it for me and I was excited. And by did it to me I mean, turned me on mentally. Excited my brain waves, made me want to read the daily paper again along with the *New York Times* and *USA Today* all so I could surprise her with my knowledge of world events.

She was mentally and physically beautiful, to me. I kept shaking my head in surprise and slight disbelief that I had met her. And that she had met me. All this was going through my head as I listened to her go on about her day at work, the ride home and eventually the getting home. I was getting use to it as this was the third day that we had been enjoying the rambling conversations of a get to know you type. I think I was so caught up in the sound of her voice as it came out of the phone and slid down my throat that I missed the actual words she was saying.

The words sliding down the back of my throat tasted sour. So I asked her to repeat what she had just said while crossing fingers and toes that I had heard incorrectly that she didn't say what I think she said.

She paused before saying "My boyfriend is getting upset. I haven't been available for him since you and I have been talking."

Did this chick just say boyfriend? No, no she couldn't have.

"I'm sorry could you repeat that, I could have sworn you said boyfriend."

"I did."

Silence buzzed on the line as my mind did all kind of twirls and tilt a whirls digesting that the woman I was planning a future with, even if she didn't know, had a man. Not a girlfriend but a man. I could have sort of dealt with the girlfriend but a man, oh hell nawl.

"You never told me you had a boyfriend or hell anyone in your life."

"I didn't think I had to, you've been on my page. I know you've checked out my profile. I'm not hiding it." she said with a slight anger tinged with a little bit of I know this girl isn't trying to check me tone. "So yeah I got a boyfriend, is this going to be a problem?"

"Uhmmm yeah that's going to be a hell of a

problem. I honestly barely looked at your profile after you added me. I'm not a Facebook fanatic. Hell I only log on once a week. Why didn't you mention this when we met at the BBQ two weeks ago?" I asked with a disbelief tinged tone.

"Because it didn't matter. I have a boyfriend so what?"

"So what? You have a BOY-friend, I am a lesbian…hello! Do you not see the issue here?"

"No I don't. My last girlfriend didn't care and he knows what I do."

"He knows!?!"

"Yes, he knows; I'm bisexual."

"Hold up bisexual doesn't mean a cheat or a freak. It just means you can love both sexes but not at the same damn time. That's hella nasty."

"You hold the hell up, I'm not nasty, a cheat or a freak. I'm a grown ass woman who handles her business. Like I said my boyfriend knows what I do and doesn't have a problem with it nor do the women I date."

"Well I'm glad we aren't dating then because I don't get down with threesomes of the before and after kind."

"Before and after what?"

"Before or after you fuck him. And on that note it's been real nice chatting with you, see you online. I have to go, my dog is jealous of the time we've been spending together and I need to go make it up to her."

That ended my walk down lover's imaginary lane. Or so I thought. Two days later I get a text message saying "hey I was thinking of you, hope you are all right."

I debated on ignoring it and her. I was still pissed off that I had started falling for someone who was as shallow and self absorbed enough to think that her profile on some web site should tell her story for her. I talked it over with friends who chastised me for not doing my due diligence after she added me or even when we exchanged numbers.

My reasoning was simple, who gives their number to someone else when they are in a relationship? Who then proceeds to go on two dates with said person and spend several evenings unwinding over the phone without mentioning that they were involved? They said a lot of folks.

Working full time and going to school full time doesn't lend much time for anything else. I know I've been out of the dating game for the last two years pursing my masters but I just didn't want to hear it was that bad.

I responded to her text because all of the women I had met before her hadn't excited me, made me think as much, feel as much. This time my little head was leading and the big head was following. We started talking again. I tried not to get to caught up, enjoying it for what it was, a mental fuck, one of the best I had ever had but still a mental fuck.

She kept pushing for us to meet up, hang out. I pushed back with just words please ma'am that's all I want, just words. That lasted for another month before I finally gave in and agreed to dinner. That was a mistake. To hear those words that I so loved coming from lips that were beautiful in their own right but surrounded by a frame that literally took my breath away. I was done, hook, line and sinker, dipped in corn meal and fried. She had me.

She had me for the next two years. She had me on a string of possibilities; of her possibly leaving him for me, maybe, one day but not this day, this hour, this minute or second. Deal with it. And I did. It wasn't like I didn't know from start right? She was his and I was the other, the side piece who wanted to be the main chick to a chick who claimed to be bisexual but only late at night when he wasn't available or at the club when she wanted to shock those who were looking.

I was happy to fill that role, til I just wasn't happy anymore. And it wasn't like she was being disrespectful when she fucked him before coming to see me, or calling him from my bed telling him she loved him while I licked her pussy. When she called out his name when she climaxed on the tip of my tongue, I didn't even bitch, didn't say one word. I signed up for this mental fuck.

And now the ride is over. One day her words didn't move me as much as before. That was the start. Then hell one day I just got grown. Simple as that. Realized I was worth more, could give more and needed more. Cut her off like a nicotine or crack habit, she was one, cold turkey via text message. "Leave me the fuck alone". She did.

That was four months ago. Got another text today, "hey I was thinking of you, hope you are all right". I passed on that hit.

Time

She's doing it, though we both pretending she's not. The several calls shared daily and the twice weekly letters help us to pretend. Pretend that the time passing is being shared by more than just words, ink and paper. We both pretend that she's on vacation, chosen a sabbatical; work has taken her off to foreign lands even. Everything but the truth.

The truth of, she's locked away. Not for a crime per se or at least not one of the ones you are thinking on and I know you're thinking "locked up!"? What did she do and that goes with that. Does it matter? She's still doing time, locked up till someone who doesn't know her, understand her or love her decides that she is no longer a danger to herself or others.

The others is what really got her locked up. Finally. When she started cutting at eleven, no one said a word really other than stop, slapped on a band aid and said be more careful. When she started talking to people at sixteen that no one could, no one said a word, did a thing. She was always odd. I mean who cuts themselves on purpose right? Crazy folks do, so talking to the wall is what crazy does. They let her. Talk to the ones no one could see, rather than talking to her.

No one said much or did much till she was

twenty-one, still living at home with her momma
and decided that momma was evil to the core and
had to be killed before she corrupted anyone else.
The people she talked to, the ones who no one saw
but her, agreed. Fortunately or unfortunately she
spoke out loud and people who really where there
heard and she was finally given the treatment she
needed. Locked up.

From what she tells me it helped. Helped her
to quiet the voices in her head, helped her to find
her place in a society where people only speak to
those who can be seen by all. A society where cuts
on your arms and legs lead to questions you really
don't want to answer anymore. Now that you
recognize, recognize crazy.

I say she told me because I met her well
after this happened. Many years, so many in fact
that those around her didn't bother to tell me
anything, warn a sister if you will. I met a "cured"
black woman, a strong black woman who appeared
to have her shit together. We fell in love.

I loved her and she loved me. So much so
that I overlooked some signs, you know not the
flashing neon light ones, just the little discount
signs you find in the back of the store. I ignored the
mini bouts of depression in what should have been
happy moments in our life. Like our first year

anniversary, she stayed home with the lights out complaining that her co-workers didn't like her anymore. She snapped out of it a few days later and I put the situation out of my memory, besides she made it up to me. That's what a good girlfriend does.

I ignored her as the bouts of depression increased till they became the norm for us. Her being depressed and staying up for three to four sometimes five days in a row, talking, planning and plotting her next move at work, in life. At first I stayed up with her, listened and even joined in. It made sense you know, maybe her coworkers were plotting against her. She was good at what she did, so good that they didn't complain much when she started not showing up at work. In those 72hrs of being constantly up she would produce like a rock star. She would work in between rages against them and society in general.

Everything was okay even when it was the neighbors against her, the guy on the corner with the kids who would run and play only in front of her stoop or the upstairs old lady with the dogs who she swore was having the dogs bark only when she slept, you know to wake her up. And then finally it was me. I was against her. That's what she told me at midnight, that I, the love of her life, was against her.

She said this in the middle of walking the familiar path between the living room and our bedroom, walked so much that the carpet had a tread pattern worn into it. At first I ignored her, really I wasn't listening. I was tired. Had been tired for the last two years. Tired of not being happy but being in love, if that makes sense. I had to love her to stay. At least that's what I told myself. Besides she needed me, I fed her, kept the bills paid and stuff. She was working, sorta. More freelance than anything by this point. Did I mention she's a terrific artist and a computer whiz?

Well she kept repeating I was against her, till I heard it. She said that I was poisoning her with the food I was cooking her every day. She even said my pussy had microbes in it that she was ingesting when she went down on me. I blinked at that one 'cause lord knows it had been some months since the last time we had something resembling sex.

She went on and on building up her case of me being against her, trying to kill her. I let her. Not really realizing that maybe this time I shouldn't have. I mean it wasn't her first rant session of the evening and I had been briefly mentioned in others but this one was strictly about me. Everything I did to her, around her, including the clothes I kept at her house, if that makes sense. She said there were electrodes in my clothing that kept her inside the house. They tracked her for me. Especially the jacket I kept on a hook by the door. That one was the one. She stared at it for what seemed like hours.

She kept repeating I wouldn't let her out till I finally said that I was going to do her one better and leave. It was two a.m. and I had reached my limit. I wasn't equipped for this shit. I told her this and some more things that had been bundled up inside as I put my shoes on and slung my purse across my shoulder. Told her I wasn't coming back either. I remember saying that over my back as I approached the door and the now infamous jacket.

That's really all I remember outside of seeing a brief picture of my hand reaching for the door knob. They told me the rest of the story when I woke up from the coma she put me in days later. I was told that she hit me from behind with something, probably one of her wooden art pieces. The first blow knocked me out but it didn't stop her from continuing to hit me. She hit me til my blood covered everything within reach, walls and floor. At least twenty times by the doctors estimate.

They found me hours later, this was only after they found her wandering the streets of our city covered in my blood. She told them that she got free from me, finally. After it was all said and done the truth came out, after the rescue of me from her apartment. After the, I'm sure, confusing questioning of her about why I was the only one bleeding, the only one hurt. The truth came out, for her and for me.

I'm still here for her, months later, slow recovery on both of our parts, me physically her mentally. They say she got off her meds and had a break, one that I should have spotted a long time ago. I said thanks. I mean what do you say to she's crazy and you should have known, should have recognized the signs. Or even worse, she didn't tell you? No one mentioned her stint years before in a psych ward, let alone her. Not even her mother who I haven't heard from since this all happened.

So we pretend. Pretend. Pretend that the time passing is being shared by more than just words, ink and paper. We both pretend that she's on vacation, chosen a sabbatical, work has taken her off to foreign lands even. Everything but the truth. She's back on her medicine and apologetic. I know she didn't mean it. Which is why I accept her phone calls. Why I answer her letters and pretend that the time passing is a happy one. It's the least I could do for the woman I loved and who loves me, the best she can, behind walls and fences.

morning

morning
afternoon
evening
love

she says
good morning
with a kiss
breast pressing down
through cotton
weighing heavily
in her decision
to leave or stay

she leaves as
my lips part

she says
I missed you
in the afternoon
with a hug
breasts pushing in
arms encircling
her scent welcoming
me home

she pulls back
as I lean in

sometimes I
need more

sometimes she
wants less
we meet in the middle
during our middle living
recapping our
day so as to
feel as if
the other was there
in the middle of our
daily living

she says good night
in the dark
pressing against my side
as if securing her life
during the night
to mine

The After

I hate the after. What do you say after the best sex you think you have ever had? Do you become the romantic cuddlier you think she wants? Do you pull back because you know this is more than you can handle? Do you let go and let whatever in?

I made a choice, consciously, subconsciously, who knows I just went with what felt right. Opened my heart and everything else to her at that exact moment, 'round midnight to the possibilities no matter what they might be. So I held her close and whispered in her ear all the things I wanted to hear.

How her skin felt like warm liquid satin to me. How I loved tangling my fingers and burying my nose in her locs, inhaling her. How I loved her natural scent mixed with the oils from her hair and the shea butter that she swears by. How I loved the way she giggled when I tickled her and the way she laughed when I said something that wasn't really funny. How when I call she answers. I do love that.

 I whispered silently how much I needed her to be the one. How much she could hurt me but that I was cool with that. I was willing to accept "some" pain in exchange for a lifetime of pleasure. Whispered in Braille how I wanted a wife and kids. The American/heterosexual dream realized except with two mommies, two kids and a dog. I was willing to compromise on the dog.

I wrote her a letter in the clouds promising to follow when she wanted to lead and to pick up the slack when she wanted to drift. All this while she fell asleep to me rubbing her back, soothing her fears and pushing into her dreams. I wanted her to dream of me, of us, of we. So I continued to whisper long after she fell asleep. I continued to rub me into her.

Memorized her skin, all the beautiful blemishes that make her her and now mine. The smattering of freckles across her back of all places. I promise to kiss each one some day. The rough patch on her knee from a bike accident when she was 13. A scar in the corner of her left eye, a reminder that little brothers grow up. All this I knew because I listened, because I love her.

Now don't get me wrong I didn't fall in love with her last night because the sex was great. No, that was just the icing on my love cake. I fell in love with her because she wants to love me.
Do you know how hard it is to love someone who doesn't want to love you? How hard is it to love someone who fights love and all that it can be and they don't even know it? Conditioned to not getting what they want they can't accept what they have been looking and asking for.

She was none of that. Clean and clear like a spring breeze. She said what she wanted, what she needed and most importantly what she was going to give. Her, all of her. How could I not love her?

So I laid back and made plans. You know the kind. Started out simple, next weekend maybe we can get away. Some little bed and breakfast in the country where no one knows us or maybe to the city of big lights and dreams realized or crushed all in a roll of the dice. In a month or two a trip to the meet my moms and the rest of those nuts that I call family. I think she's going to like her. I think they are going to like each other.

A ceremony one day with friends and family. Kids one day, a family, our family. Did the whole "_____ and _____" kissing in a tree song and dance. The thought made me giggle out loud. She woke but only to mumble what I think, what I pray was I love you before kissing me lightly and falling promptly back to sleep. Considered doing something else, anything else so that she would do it again and again and again.

touches

she tells me
I can
touch her

just not
here, here
and there

not because
she doesn't like it
when I've
attempted
in the past

to touch her
here, here
and there

it's just that
touches
here, here
and there
bring back
memories
that she's still
processing

flash backs of
pictures
polaroid's
snapshots

of pain
at an age
when she was
still learning
that two
plus three
is five
and that sing
alongs in class
were not going
to last much
longer

she's still processing

how momma
didn't know
how momma
still don't know
and how he
how he
pretends he
doesn't know
didn't do
smiles and touches
whispered warnings
shaped her
into she

who tells me
I can touch
her

just not
here, here
and there

here, here
and there
changes…

Tic-tac-toe

We played tic-tac-toe on a rainy Saturday afternoon. I wanted to be quiet and still, thinking on a nap. She wanted to do something, anything as long as it involved me. I wanted to stay in bed, with as little on as possible, napping between bites of whatever I found in the kitchen or that she brought in to tease me from sleep. As a compromise, I suggested in bed tic-tac-toe with a twist. For every O placed on the paper either a kiss was given or an article of clothing was taken off. For every X placed, a body part any part could be licked. She grinned before grabbing a notepad and pen off the bedside table handing both to me with an air of anticipation.

I chose X, first.

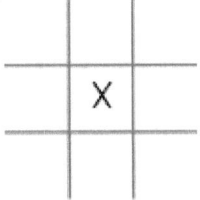

She watched me, anticipating where the first kiss would go, I leaned over and licked her bottom lip. No sucking, no biting, just a small lick. Surprised her I could tell, surprised her enough that she followed my lick of her lip by doing the same, licking her lip that is with the tip of her tongue as she carefully placed her first **0**.

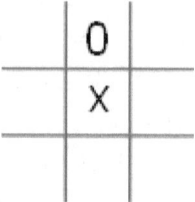

I waited to see which she would choose, a kiss or clothing. She chose my purple t-shirt, borrowed from her this morning after my shower. I gave it willingly, knowing that it smelled of me and her. She loved to sniff for me when I wasn't around. She wrapped it around her neck, holding the end up to her nose.

I placed my X in a nice little line beside the other, while staring at her as she smiled and licked her lips a second time. Suggestion.

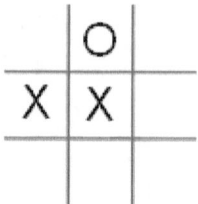

I chose a more interesting pathway. Instead of her lips I reached over and pulled up her t-shirt, freeing her double-d's to my view. Never been a breast woman til I met her. How could you not love these perfect globes. I loved the heaviness as I held them each in one hand. As I separated them and licked slowly in the valley between them, tasting the slight saltysweet of her, while feeling the heat of her skin rise up to meet me. I flattened my tongue as I approached her throat, turning my head slightly not stopping til I reached the top or the bottom depending on how you look at things. I pulled back and watched her, eyes closed chest thrust out. She enjoyed. After a few seconds she recovered enough to pull her shirt back down and place her O, blocking me.

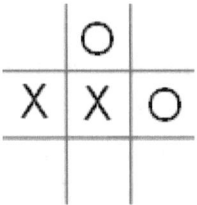

Again I waited, this time she took a kiss. A long lingering one that lasted much longer than my casual lick. Her shirt was pulled up once again and we were skin to skin, the notepad sticking me in the back reminded me that we were playing a game. A game I wanted to win and I wasn't going out this easily.

I placed my X while contemplating what I wanted to taste next. Strategy.

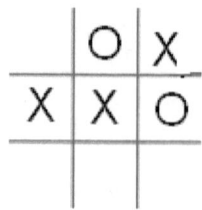

"Open your legs", I told her.

"What?" she asked, slightly startled.

"Open your legs" I responded with a slight shove as her back hit the bed.

She did slowly while staring at me with the look she gets when I'm about to take her there. You know where there is..over the top. I slowly lowered my head, inhaling her scent all while realizing she was wet and waiting on me. I lowered my head, nose leading me to where I wanted to be on a rainy Saturday. I licked the inside of her thighs first, in the upper right corner, the ticklish spot. Even bit down slightly, reminding her of games we play. I heard her breath catch as the skin grew taunt in between my teeth. Natural reaction to pull away but she knows not to and her skin instantly relaxed. I thought I heard a mumbled "I'm sorry". We would discuss that later, for now the game we were playing was going forward and I planned on winning. Winning it all.

I continued to lick her thighs intermingled

with little bites as I played tag with her clit. Visually watching it rise to attention and beg for my attention. I did. One lick, from bottom to tip. One lick down and then I paused. I mean really per the game rules I was only allowed one lick right? She wasn't protesting the game changes. Hips thrusting upwards in agreement. Begging me with her body to continue to lick and I did. Licked and sucked her clit, lips and her pussy. Tongue deep inside, as she rode me slightly from the prone position, thighs clenching when I finally got my fingers involved. They went inside while my tongue played more on the outside, debating which had more fun. Either way.

Game over, Kat got the kitty…

If you are my Facebook friend then you've read the following...still wanted to share. *Jokes*

Top 10 Rules for Being a Lesbian

I've met so many women new to the life who have no clue what "the life" is about. So I figured why not help them and future others with a top 10 list ala Kat. Now I caution you dear readers to NOT take these to heart. Please apply common sense and logic to your life and situations.

10. Most studs/masculine oriented women are short. It's the rule. Sorry to say there's nothing you can do about it because most women stopped growing at 15. I think Air Jordans elevate you an inch or two, buy her a pair. Please not on the second date.

9. Dating women isn't the same as dating men. Contrary to popular belief just because she wears jerseys and kicks doesn't mean she's handy with a hammer or that she can lift more than you. On the flip side just because she thinks heels go with everything and that flip flops are for children under 12 doesn't mean she can cook and clean. So do you and let her do her as well. Recognize who you are with and leave the stereotypes outside with the trash.

8. Learn the lingo. How else can you grow as a certified card carrying lesbian? We are family is not just a song. The children aren't just the ones you gave birth to and being called bitch by one of the boys is rather normal. Don't bother cursing them back because it's a waste of time once they start doing the twirls, round the worlds and getting louder with each word and dance move.

7. Most people have already figured out your a lesbian so there's no need to take an ad out in your church bulletin. You might as well just give to the building fund directly. While there ask when they plan on breaking ground because by my estimation they should have about half a million socked away. My grandmother thinks it more. Also having a same sex roommate in a one bedroom apartment at the tender age of 45 isn't really saving money. Granny told me to tell you to quit playing.

6. Don't fall in love and "attempt" to marry the first chick that smiles at you. Yes, I know she's your soul mate and the reason why you breathe but please don't announce marriage plans after being together for four months. Most lesbians smile while taking bets on whether or not this will occur. I generally place $50 on not. I love you like a step-cousin but gas is high.

5. Date who you like. Fem on fem action is sexy. Stud on stud action is sexy. Get over it people and quit believing the hype of only opposites attracting. Personally I think you should date someone who holds the same interests as you. If that's fishing and ESPN go for it.

4. Lesbian U-haul is a real and common occurrence and most of us will experience it at least once. See rule 6. I have yet to figure out how you leave with less than what you arrived with. Nor have I figured out who gets to keep the pets or the really cool toys. Yeah the toys...hmmm

3. A year long lesbian relationship is cause for celebration. Unfortunately the couple will more than likely have a fight en route to the party and break up. This will still lead to a quiet celebration among some of the party attendees. Pay close attention to any ex's and recently acquired "new" friends.

2. If you are femme then your best friend can not be a stud and vice versa. People will assume you are dating or sleeping together. Stupid but true. Both of you will field numerous well intended questions on your status with the added disclaimer of I/we see you together so much. Also don't appear to be overly friendly when you are hanging out. In other words ixnay the dancing together and whispering in each other's ear and please for the love of all things holy don't eventually date. You are the reason this rule is in place.

1. If she tells you that she's still in love with her ex but wants to get to know you RUN!!! You will be the band-aid that licks her wounds while she secretly licks her ex. Now mind you I'm not saying you can't cure her heartache but why should you? Time heals all wounds so give her some before you end up with some new fresh ones

Remember ladies..these are just jokes! Well unless they apply to you..lol

The 11 Lesbians you will meet in your lifetime...

Disclaimer: This was in response to "The Eight Black Gays you will meet in your lifetime". It's all in fun. Seriously..lol Adding as they come to me..feel free to give me some "titles".

The Professional Stud:

She doesn't work but always is dressed from head to toe in whatever is popular at the moment, has more pairs of kicks than the shoe store and more tattoos than Lil Wayne. Her job is to be the hood stereotypical male. If she could get you preggers and bounce on you she would. Instead she just lays on your couch, watching your TV, eating your food, smoking herb and texting the five other women in her life on the cell phone you purchased for her.

Pro: She's good in bed...maybe and she knows where the best parties are at.
Con: Everything above

The Professional lesbian:

She's usually beautiful and femmed up from head to toe with nails, weave and five inch heels all on point. She doesn't work because McDonalds requires a hair net and besides she feels you should pay for the privilege of being her woman or "studsband". She lays on your couch, flipping your channels, polishing her nails, changing her wig/weave out daily and texting the next chick on the phone you purchased her.

Pro: She looks good on your arm
Con: All of the above AND she's a pillow princess

The Natural Lesbian:

She's been a vegan for all of five days but still looks down on you for eating meat or sugar or hell anything that takes heat to cook. She backslides every now and then with a pork-chop sandwich when she visits her grandmother. She visits her grandmother every week. She burns incense all day and douses you in herbs and oils to purify your essence. Wearing a bra and deodorant is optional in her world. Everyone is her sista including all the ones she sleeping with.

Pro: She'll make you a mean salad
Con: She won't believe you when you tell her she smells

The I'm fighting Jesus to love you Lesbian:

After church on Sunday you might as well move out til Wednesday because it's going to take that long for her to get over the fact that she is sinning and will be burning a slow death in her version of hell for loving you. Mind you she has five kids from three different men and was screwing anything that moved by age 15, plus that stint in county for check fraud but that won't put her in the hell house like loving you will.

Pro: She's probably good in bed, crazy usually is
Con: You'll have to pray and ask for forgiveness after sex and deal with all them damn kids

The I'm new to the life lesbian:

No one wants to be with her because she's new and we are all scared she's going to go back to dick. She's always in the club, eyes wide open, staring in shock as women touch each other in public.

Pro: She's new to the life
Con: She's new to the life

The regular lesbian:

She's all right, goes to work, takes care of the kids and house. Has good credit and can cook some mean greens or change a tire in under 15 minutes. She still trying to please her momma who thinks one day she won't be gay anymore. Baby daddy is still in the picture as well because she was such a good woman, you know outside of the lesbian thing.

Pro: She loves professional studs or professional lesbians
Con: She needs some self esteem lessons

The rainbow lesbian:

This chick so damn gay she makes you cringe. Everything is a LGBTQ fight, march or rally. She makes Martin Luther King look like he didn't do ish but watch wrestling on Saturday mornings. You say hi and she responds with " I'm gay". Every person she meets she comes out to and dares them not to accept it.

Pro: We need folks like her in the community
Con: She dates natural lesbians and believes
she doesn't smell either

The Pillow Princess

Well............she's never tasted pussy, has no desire to and hopes you understand.

Pro: I can't find one
Con: Isn't it obvious?

The Touch Me Not Stud:

She feels weak and womanly when she climaxes so won't let you taste or touch her. Rarely will you ever see her totally naked. On the flip side she'll do you all day long.

Pro: She got a mean head game
Con: She's fucking dudes on the side

The Bisexual Lesbian:

She's really bi but can't/won't tell because that would lead to no dates 'cause you know "real" lesbians don't date bisexuals.

Pro: Generally she's not a bad chick, you know outside of the lying to herself and others.
Con: Jim might be more than a friend.

Transgender Lesbian:

S/he's finding himself and can't understand why you don't understand and why you not jumping up and down with joy at that newly grown beard.

Pro: S/he's very well versed on the medical side of things like insurance and hospitals.
Con: S/he got a damn beard and sound like your daddy.

Again just jokes folks..please no hate mail! Love mail only to anondra.kat.williams@gmail.com

Please enjoy an excerpt from my upcoming novel **"Pat Greene"**. Scheduled for release in the fall of 2014

Pat Greene

Some women just aren't meant to love, I wasn't one of them. I loved hard and deep, unfortunately I tended to love those women that just weren't meant to love. Either that or they didn't love me. I didn't dwell on the second part of that too much. I was busy loving, loving on every sista who shined their big pearly whites at me. Loving every sista who said the she loved me back, with eyes closed and head turned sideways. It's best to do that when you lie. Except my eyes were open and I saw the lie but I believed the words. I know you going who does that? Well, hell I do obviously and I am she, the one who is going to share the loves of her life. And baby when I tell you I've had more than a few, lawd there should be a sin against loving so many women, wrong ones and right ones.

I'm Pat Greene by the way, nice to meet you. My mother, Bessie Mae Greene, of the Mississipi Greene's, named me Patricia but that's just a 'lil to fussy for me and besides I'm just a 'lil to country to be going around with all that stuck on me. My momma was always trying to be better than and there ain't nothing wrong with that, I just happen to be content with all right for now and we can maybe do better later.

Hell, that might explain all the wrong women. I was constantly looking at right now and thinking they or it was going to improve.

They mainly didn't and if they did it was after they left me. Now ain't that some shit. I put up with all that mess, teaching you how to properly love a woman and you go and do it for the next one with no thanks to lil 'ol Pat, sitting over her all on her lonesome.

Never fear though, I wasn't never alone for long. A so called friend suggested I should wait between relationships, give myself time to heal. I told her to go on with that mess. I needs a woman in the here and now not in whatever future she talking about. Besides by the time I'm done with a woman I'm already healing. She done cut and bruised me up till there ain't nothing left to do but to heal. I've also found that burning up her clothes really makes the healing that much better. Try it.

Like I said, I'm Pat and I'm here to tell you the story of me. Maybe you'll learn something, maybe you won't. That ain't really up to me, now is it?

Pat Green
Joe

Most of my women thought I was fine and I guess that kept them coming around me, like bees to honey. I'm sweet and easy like a cold class of ice tea on hot day in Hot Coffee, Mississippi. I keep myself looking good, sugar sharp they say. I'm dressed to the nines plus one every time I step out the door. Looking like a proper lady, that part of my momma's teaching stuck. I don't get these young girls and boy's walking around here like they just rolled off the couch. Either their underwear showing cause they pants so low or theirs shorts up to their ass crack, shoes raggedy and these piss poor excuses for wigs. My po momma and grandmomma would turn over in their grave and I can't blame them one bit.

Though being honest my granny would probably laugh. She had a good laugh and found most folks funny. I think I get my sense of humor from her. "Child", she would say, "you have to laugh sometimes when the world around you is going crazy, laugh and shake it off. The sun gonna rise and the moon gonna set. You just have to deal with the living in between time. "

So I do or rather I did. I'm not long for this world or so them overpriced doctors say. I say the only one that's going to tell me when it's time for me to go is me and my father above. We ain't spoke in a while, I ain't called and he ain't either so I'm guessing we both good.

Don't get me wrong I do believe in preparing for things in life. I could get hit by a bus tomorrow, that's how Johnnie Mae died. She's half blind with her glasses on and trying to be cute decided to leave them at home and go shopping downtown. Foolishness, I tell you just foolishness.

She did have a nice home going though. There was a room full of folks talking about how good and gracious and kind she was. People sure do lie at funerals. I kept my mouth shut and sent her on her way the way I know she would have appreciated. I poured out a little liquor when I left. That boy Tupac thought he was the first to do that. We been doing that, though not as much as he did. That's a waste and we don't waste 'nan drop of liquor around here.

So anyway I've been sick for the last year or two and its starting to drag me down, don't get out as much as I want to anymore. There ain't much to see but I do miss hanging with the women in my group. The card parties and gossip, always some gossip. I think I miss that the most. Who dating who, who done moved so in so in, who done broke up and who is pregnant.

Now that last one always made for interesting guessing. If you haven't figured it out by now I'm what they call a lesbian. In my day we called it being a dyke or hell nothing at all. Getting pregnant was always good gossip amongst women who preferred women. I never had kids, wanted them of course but just couldn't go about doing it the way you had to back then. Now you can get pregnant with a turkey baster. Though I'm thinking the other way just sounds a little bit better to me, a little more pleasant and all. Besides I always wanted to ask them did they reuse the baster? Keep it in the closet as a little special something or other, you know memories and shit.

I'm digressing. Honey I swear I can get caught up in the little things. Speaking of small things, do you remember your first kiss? I remember mine clear as day. Little girl by the name of Joe, Her name was Josephine but it didn't fit her any better than Patricia fit me. She came up to me in the second grade and said I was going to be hers and followed it up with a kiss. She missed my lips but that don't matter. I still see Joe every now and then. She got a passel of bad ass grandkids and great grandkids with her at all times. She looks happy.

I tell everyone Joe, turned me gay, if she hadn't kissed me ain't no telling where I would be at right now or what I would be doing. They all laugh. You can't turn no one gay but it's still a funny joke. I've been using that one for 70 years now.

Joe was the first of many girls that kissed me and that I kissed back. Oh yeah right around the 6th grade I went and gave Joe, that kiss back and honey let me tell you, I didn't miss a lip. No ma'am not that time nor the next few times after.

"Pat Greene" coming in the fall of 2014

ABOUT THE AUTHOR

Many thanks to all for reading "SistaGirl" my second book. If you haven't please check out my first foray into writing "black girl love" available in both e-book and paperback.

For those who don't know anything about me I am a writer, poet, radio host and all around lover of words. My work is currently featured in the anthologies "Life, Love & Lust 1 & 2" a collection of short stories & "Her Voice" a collection of poetry. I will be in the soon to be released "Geechee to Gumbo: Black Southern Womanloving Culture & Politics" and "G.R.I.T.S : Girls Raised In The South- An Anthology on Southern Queer Womyns' Voices and Their Allies".

In 2009 I started Shades Retreat: Personal, You. Shades Retreat is a empowerment, growth and change retreat for queer women of color. Shades Retreat occurs once a year during the third week of April. Join us…www.shadesretreat.org

You can connect with me @ www.anondrawilliams.com or send me an email anondra.kat.williams@gmail.com

NOTES:

Anondra Williams